ARSENIC AND YOUNG LACY

A Marcia Banks and Buddy Mystery

Kassandra Lamb
author of the Kate Huntington Mysteries

Arsenic and Young Lacy
A Marcia Banks and Buddy Mystery

Published in the United States of America by **misterio press**,
a Florida limited liability company
http://misteriopress.com

~~~~~~~~~~~~

Edited by Marcy Kennedy

Cover and interior design by Melinda VanLone, Book Cover Corner

Photo credits: silhouette of woman and dog by Majivecka
(right of use purchased from dreamstime.com)

ISBN 13: 978-0-9974674-1-3 (misterio press LLC)
ISBN 10: 10: 0-9974674-1-X

*To our courageous and dedicated combat veterans,
who all too often come home wounded
physically and/or mentally.*

CHAPTER ONE

"Mar-ci-a," the frustrated voice coming out of my phone emphasized every syllable of my name. "What the *devil* have you gotten yourself into now?"

The voice was that of my, uh, boyfriend ... um, male friend... man friend... lover?

Hmm, tall, hunky Will Haines definitely wasn't a boy, and male friend sounded way too platonic. Man friend was kind of primitive–brought up some interesting images of us taking turns hauling each other off to some cave. My nether regions sat up and panted.

Sadly, we did not qualify for lover status yet, although it hadn't been for lack of trying, at least recently.

"What do you mean?" I feigned my most innocent tone, and crossed my fingers to boot. Did people still do that? Ever since Will had pointed out that I wasn't a typical thirty-something, I'd been second guessing myself all over the place.

The sound of air being blown out in a long-suffering sigh. "Why am I getting a BOLO on some guy for a destruction of property charge and your name's on it as the complainant, with some address up in Ocala? *And* it's flagged that the suspect is potentially dangerous."

Crapola. I hadn't realized a be-on-the-lookout bulletin in Ocala would make it all the way to Sheriff Will's desk in Collinsville, a whole county away.

"I was... helping out a friend."

Rainey Bryant wasn't a friend exactly, although she thought she was. She was my client, or rather the client of the agency for which I train service dogs. And technically it would probably be unethical for me to become friends with her, although she seemed to want that to happen.

Yeah, I know, I'm a mess in the relationship department.

Buddy, my Black Lab-Rottie mix, whined softly and tilted his head at me with his patented what's-up look. I'd been about to take him for a walk, had the leash in my hand even, when Will called.

"Just a minute, boy."

"You talking to me?" Will said.

"No, to Buddy."

"Are you *going* to talk to me?"

"Yeah, I'm just trying to figure out what to say."

"How about the truth."

Ouch!

"That's not fair," I said. "When have I ever lied to you?"

Another sigh. "Your sins tend to be more ones of omission."

Okay, I had to give him that. "Look, it's a long story."

"I've got nothing better to do right now."

I held my hand out, palm parallel to the floor and motioned down. Buddy cocked his head the other way, then laid down. I flopped back on my sofa.

"Okay, but this has to do with a client so some of it's confidential. You have to keep it to yourself." I paused for breath before plunging in.

~~~

I really liked Rainey Bryant from the first time I met her. Although later, I would wonder why.

She was bright, with a friendly smile and short blonde hair bracketing an attractive face. And despite all that she'd been through, there was an innocent, child-like quality about her.

And she'd been through plenty. For starters, she was an Army nurse so she'd survived basic training, although perhaps hers wasn't as rigorous physically as that of a woman who'd volunteered for the infantry.

I didn't know, since I wasn't totally up on how such things worked inside the military. I was pretty familiar, however, with how things worked, or didn't, after people got out of the military.

The service dogs I train for veterans who suffer from PTSD should be like a prosthesis or a wheelchair for physical injuries, paid for by the Veterans Administration. But they aren't always. Fortunately, the agency I train for has some grant money for scholarships.

Rainey didn't know that I knew that she was the recipient of one of those scholarships. Mattie Jones, the director of the agency, had accidentally let it slip.

I'd met Rainey for the first time when I took her potential service dog to her house to introduce them to each other. It was something Mattie insisted on–make sure the animal and recipient are compatible before starting the expensive training process.

At that point, I was officially Lacy's foster mom. Mattie had arrangements with several local rescue shelters that allowed her trainers to take dogs on a trial basis.

Lacy, a white Collie-Alaskan Husky mix, was a little yappy, but otherwise she had the right temperament for a service animal–intelligent, people-oriented, eager to please.

Rainey loved her at first sight. So much so that she turned me down when I offered a little while later to get her a more protective breed, a German Shepherd perhaps.

The offer had been in response to her revelation that she'd been sexually assaulted by a male soldier during her second deployment in Afghanistan. And now her greatest fear in life was being assaulted again.

The guy was a non-com and she was an officer, but still the Army had claimed it was her word against his whether or not the sex had been consensual. She'd developed PTSD symptoms and was shipped home early with a medical discharge. She'd been devastated, not only by the assault, but by the sense of betrayal when the organization she'd planned to devote her life to had let her down.

Having heard plenty on the news about the problems with sexual assault in the military, I believed her. And my heart went out to her.

Fast-forward three and a half months, and Lacy was now a fully trained service dog. It was time for me to deliver her to her new owner and start the human phase of the training process. This usually takes from two to three weeks, with some breaks in there for me to attend to my other trainees. Forget about having a life during that time—which could now be added to the list of things that kept confounding Will's and my efforts to consummate our relationship.

The first time I went to Ocala to train with Rainey Bryant, it was a beautiful, sunny morning. Not unusual for spring in central Florida, and a pleasant contrast to the April showers—translation: damp and dreary—of my native Maryland.

~~~

"Come on, Marcia," Will said. "I'm growing old here."

"I thought you said you didn't have anything better to do." I lowered my voice to what I hoped was a sultry whisper. "I could come down there and keep you occupied, big boy."

Yet another sigh. "Client. Lacy. Sunny day."

"Okay, okay."

I felt an attack of the guilts for talking about Rainey's history, even though she seemed to talk about it freely enough herself. But Will needed to know in order to understand Rainey, and why this whole stalking thing was pretty serious.

"Remember, this is all confidential."

"If it will make you feel any better, the assault would have come up in a background check on this woman anyway."

Warmth spread through my chest. This man understood me so well.

~~~

I was really, really excited about showing Rainey what Lacy

could do. In addition to all the normal commands and behaviors that helped PTSD sufferers, such as the dog waking her owner up to interrupt a nightmare, I had come up with one that was unique to Rainey's situation.

I'd created a maneuver that I'd dubbed the Lassie response. If Rainey was attacked, she could tell the dog to "Run!" and Lacy would take off and search for a passerby who could be enticed to return with the dog to help her owner.

I knew the odds were small that the dog would bring back help in a timely manner, but maybe the belief that a rescue was possible would keep Rainey from wasting her life away in a state of helplessness and fear.

Service dogs aren't the cure-all for PTSD, but they help a lot, and the hope for normalcy that they represent is, in itself, a powerful thing.

I pulled up in front of the house my client shared with her older sister. It was a modest, cement block bungalow, painted white, with dormers in a light green metal roof.

When Rainey answered my knock, her blue eyes skittered from me to the street behind me and back again. Her face was pale, and her hand trembled as she raised it to brush back an errant strand of blonde hair.

"What's the matter?" I said. Lacy looked up at me in response to my sharp tone.

Rainey waved a hand in the air in a vague gesture. "Nothing. I'm fine. Come on back."

I followed her through a sparsely furnished but spotlessly clean living room to an equally clean kitchen. Lacy bounced along beside me in her red service dog vest.

A tanned, redheaded young woman, in white slacks and a snug navy knit top, rose from a chair at the table and slid a purse strap onto her shoulder. "I'll get going then," she said to Rainey.

No Southern accent. Yet another transplant from the cold North.

The two women hugged and I heard murmuring. "So sorry…

Call you."

When they pulled apart, Rainey introduced the other woman as her friend, Carrie Williams.

Hand thrust forward, Carrie gave me a toothy smile.

I shook the proffered hand.

Then before I could react, she'd dropped into a crouch and stretched her arms out. "Oh, is this your new dog?" she squealed.

I took a half step, inserting my jeans clad leg between her and Lacy. "Sorry, she's on duty now."

Carrie stood up, frowning. "I can't pet her?"

I mustered a smile. "Not today. Once she and Rainey are working as a team, you can pet her, when she's off duty. Right now it might confuse her." I wasn't the least bit worried about the dog. But I wanted to establish the boundary up front that Lacy was not to be treated as a pet.

Carrie's attractive face settled into a not-so-attractive pout.

Rainey spared me from further discussion by taking her friend's arm and walking her toward the front door.

She was back in a moment and we went out into a large, fenced backyard.

I began to show her the various commands that Lacy knew, but Rainey seemed distracted–fidgeting and staring off into space. I hadn't even gotten to the Lassie response when I spotted tears trickling down her cheeks.

"Are you okay?"

She nodded, then shook her head. "It's him."

"Him who?"

"There's this guy. He's stalking me."

I sucked in my breath. "Do you know who it is?"

This time, she shook her head, then nodded. I resisted the urge to roll my eyes.

"It might be this guy I dated awhile back. My sister thought she saw him running away."

"Running away from what, where?"

She motioned for me to follow and walked around to the far

side of the house. She flung her hand up in the air.

The wall of the house was sprayed with big red letters.

I'LL GET YOU, BIT...

The top of the T ran off the side of the house. Assessing how much room was available for one's message was apparently not one of this vandal's strengths.

Around the second-floor window, under the peak of the roof, was a crude target, the big red bull's eye smack in the middle of the window glass itself.

"That's m...my room," Rainey said in a shaky voice.

A car crunched to a stop in the street on the other side of the six-foot privacy fence.

Rainey startled and took several steps away from the fence.

A car door slammed.

She bolted for the backyard.

I followed, wondering what exactly had triggered the flashback that had apparently taken hold of my client's mind.

She'd slithered in under the steps leading down from her back porch and had pulled Lacy in with her.

I crouched down. The white of the dog's coat stood out in the dim and dingy space. Cobwebs hung from the bottom of each wooden step. Lacy looked out at me, confusion and a touch of fear in her dark eyes.

"It's okay, girl." I gestured for her to lie down.

She tilted her chin down in what looked for all the world like a nod, then dropped onto the ground.

I was contemplating how to lure Rainey out when her sister barreled through the back door and onto the porch. Her gaze slid right past me as she scanned the backyard.

She was thinner than Rainey's average build, and she wasn't aging well. Her tie-dyed tee shirt and jeans hung loosely on her frame. Shoulder-length, stringy hair blew around her head. I noticed a few gray hairs scattered amongst the blonde ones.

"Rainey, where are you?" she called out, but low, like she was trying not to let her voice carry too far. "Why'd you call the cops?"

Then she turned, saw me and bolted back inside.

What the H?

The few short conversations I'd had with Rainey's sister had led me to believe she was a sane person. A bit of a crunchy granola type, but rational. Now I wasn't so sure.

Under the steps, Rainey put a finger to her lips in a shh gesture and shook her head. Hadn't she heard her sister go back inside?

Deciding that their dysfunctional family dynamics were none of my business, I stood up, my knees popping a little, and headed around the corner to the gate on the other side of the house. I wanted to know what was going on out front, with all the car doors slamming and such.

I got there in time to see an elderly woman walking toward the house next door and a young male sheriff's deputy headed up Rainey's front walk.

He glanced over, then veered in my direction. "Ma'am, we have a report of possible vandalism here. Can you tell me anything about it?"

I opened my mouth, but suddenly Rainey was at my elbow. "It's no biggie, Officer. They sprayed some paint on the side of her house. But I'm sure it was just some kids."

Her house? Who's her?

"Deputy, ma'am." He tipped his hat slightly and smiled. The correction and the gesture had a well-practiced feel to them.

"Who called it in?" Rainey asked, her tone sharper than it should be when talking to the law.

The deputy pointed toward the neighbor's house. "Apparently she can see the paint from her bedroom window." He gave me a hard look.

I shook my head a little. What the heck was going on here?

"I got the impression, ladies," his gaze flicked from me to Rainey, "that there might be some resistance on your part to reporting it, so she called it in herself."

Huh?

I glanced toward the gate. Rainey had left it open, and Lacy was trotting across the lawn toward us. "Come, girl." She came to me and touched her nose against my outstretched palm–the basic signal that reinforces the connection between service dog and handler. "Sit." She plopped her haunches down next to me.

When I tuned in again to the conversation, my mouth dropped open.

Rainey was giving *my* name as the owner of *her* house, carefully spelling my first name so the deputy could write it down on his little pad.

CHAPTER TWO

"So where did the 'could be dangerous' part come from?" Will asked.

I shook my head, even though Will couldn't see me. "From me, I'm afraid."

~~~

When I finally found my voice, I pointed out that a target on one's window was hardly a kids' prank.

"Did anyone see this guy?" the deputy asked.

Rainey and I spoke at the same time.

"No," she said.

"Yes." I scowled at her.

She narrowed her eyes back at me, her mouth pressed into a grim line. "Uh, my friend thought she might have gotten a glimpse of him. She's inside. I'll get her."

What friend? Carrie? She had left already.

Rainey made a gesture toward me–hand partway up, palm out–that I read to mean she didn't want me to follow. I was pretty sure that was more about her not wanting the deputy inside the house.

This was getting stranger and stranger, but I went along for now. I didn't want to inadvertently cause my client a problem. At least not until she'd had a chance to explain all this to me.

"Why didn't the Ocala Police Department respond?" I asked the deputy, to fill the awkward silence.

He gave me a strange look. "You're outside the city limits."

"Oh."

No wonder the strange look. He must be wondering why I didn't know where my own house was. I opted to let the awkward silence stretch out after that.

Rainey finally returned. "My friend has a migraine but she said the guy was six-foot, medium build, with blond hair and blue eyes." She gestured to the street. "He ran off that way."

The deputy wrote in his notepad. "Did she say what he was wearing?"

Rainey crossed her arms over her chest, then uncrossed them. "Jeans and a red jacket."

I was pretty sure she was making that part up, especially since it was in the eighties, not exactly jacket weather.

The deputy turned to me, glanced at his pad. "So Marsha, do you know this guy? How dangerous do you think he is?"

"It's Mar-see-a, Deputy. Not Marsha."

I glared at Rainey.

Her eyes were wide and red-rimmed, and her lower lip trembled. She was terrified, but of what?

"No, I don't know his name," I said. "But I think he might be dangerous."

Rainey's eyes bore into mine.

"He…he's been stalking me," I said.

It took another fifteen minutes to get rid of the deputy. He insisted on walking all the way around the house, and he took pictures of the red letters and the target on the window.

Once he was gone, I turned to Rainey, hands on hips. "What was all that about?"

She covered her face with her hands and burst into tears.

I waited patiently for her to get control of herself. Since I wasn't real sure what she was upset about, other than the stalker that is, I was clueless as to how to offer comfort.

Lacy whined softly from where she sat beside my feet. I touched the top of her head and she quieted.

Finally, I put a hand on Rainey's still shaking shoulder.

Her hands dropped from her tear-streaked face and she lunged, almost knocking me off my feet as she wrapped her arms around me in a tight hug. "Thank you so much for going along with me."

I gently extracted myself from the bear hug.

She swiped at her cheeks with the backs of her hands and sniffed loudly. "You see, my sister hates the police. She's kind of a throwback to the sixties."

"The sixties? She wasn't even born then, was she?"

"Oh no," she shook her head vigorously. "But she's into all that stuff–organic food, and... you know." She looked away, made a show of searching through her pockets.

The light finally blinked on in my attic. Her sister had drugs in the house. That's why she wanted nothing to do with the police.

Having finally found a tissue, Rainey blew her nose. "She's a bit older than me. We had different fathers."

~~~

"You probably shouldn't be telling me about the drugs part," Will said.

"I'm just guessing, and most likely it's only marijuana."

"Which is still illegal in this state."

Ignoring that comment, I lifted my long auburn hair–Will calls it red–off the back of my neck. It might technically be spring, but today the high temperature was supposed to be eighty-eight.

"Hey, how come you're just now getting the BOLO? All this happened yesterday morning."

Will sighed again, but this time I was pretty sure his frustration wasn't aimed at me.

"The printer hooked to the statewide system was probably the prototype from when computers were first invented. It works when it feels like it. The Marion County sheriff usually sends me a courtesy email, to make sure I get his BOLOs. So sometimes there's a delay."

Will frequently complained about the county commissioners, who expected him to provide twenty-first-century protection to their small rural county but refused to give him a budget that would allow him to upgrade his twentieth-century equipment.

"Hey, wait a minute," he said. "This doesn't say anything about stalking."

Okay, that irked me. "When will law enforcement start taking stalking seriously?"

"Don't get worked up. If the BOLO says the guy is dangerous, then the deputy definitely noted the stalking. The sheriff probably forgot to put that in his email. Hey, didn't Rainey say her sister thought it was her ex-boyfriend she saw?"

"Yeah."

"So she does know who he is."

"Crapola," I said. "Yeah, she does."

"Get her to tell you his name."

"I'll try."

"What does that mean?" Will asked.

"Um, you'd have to know Rainey to understand."

~~~

Rainey Bryant was very likeable, most of the time, but she could also be quite frustrating.

After her meltdown and all the hoopla with the deputy, she had brightened and insisted she wanted to take me out to lunch.

The first thing that flashed through my mind was how could a woman who needs a scholarship be so loose with money? But of course, I couldn't say that, since I wasn't supposed to know that she'd qualified for a scholarship.

And this woman supposedly had agoraphobia, which usually meant house-bound.

She must have read the skepticism on my face. "I'm okay if I'm with somebody else. It's going out alone that I mostly can't handle." She glanced down at Lacy, who was panting quietly and looking from one to the other of the human faces above her. "Is it okay to go out in public with Lacy at this point?"

Part of me wanted to get on with our interrupted training, but maybe a little break here would be good, to let Rainey recuperate from the whole stalking/flashback/police thing. My stomach rumbled, voting for lunch now instead of later. "Yeah, but she'll still be oriented to me as her handler."

Rainey nodded, a little too vigorously. "Sure, that's okay."

Even though restaurants are required to allow service dogs to enter with their owners, I preferred to find places with outdoor seating, especially this time of year when the weather's so nice.

Rainey knew of a Mexican place not far from her house.

We went in my small SUV, since I had the dog safety strap hooked up in the backseat. "You'll need to get one of these," I said as I clipped it onto the ring on Lacy's vest.

I pulled my head out of the backseat to find Rainey staring into space. I cleared my throat. "Did you get a crate for her yet?"

"Oh, yeah, yeah. Sunny found one at a yard sale."

"Sunny?" I opened my door and slid into the driver's seat.

Rainey got in on the passenger's side. "My sister. Her name's Sunshine."

My eyebrows arched up before I could catch myself. I'd never heard the sister's name before. She'd been introduced and referred to only as "my sister."

"She changed it legally awhile back," Rainey said.

Since I'd rarely seen her sister smile, the snarky part of me wanted to say that she should've changed her name to Cloudy, but I kept that thought to myself.

At the restaurant, I braced for the usual dance I have to do with hostesses and business owners. I pointed to Lacy's red vest, with *service animal* printed on it in big black letters, and opened my mouth.

The hostess flashed a bright smile. "*No problemo.*" She led us to a table in one corner of the café's patio.

We settled in, Lacy at my feet.

"It's not always that easy," I said. "Usually you'll get resistance to letting the dog in. People cannot legally ask you what your disability is, but they can ask what services the dog performs. You'll want to give some thought to how much you're willing to share with strangers."

"Oh, I don't care what people know about me."

That didn't surprise me. Rainey tended to err in the direction of TMI.

Except with the police, that is. There she was a little too free with other people's information.

"Still, you'll want a short answer ready or you'll spend your life explaining about service dogs. Something like, 'she alerts me to the approach of strangers' or 'she helps me with anxiety issues.' That one tends to stop the questions. People don't want to hear about other people's anxi–"

"I don't have anxiety *issues*." She sounded mildly offended.

I kept my mouth from dropping open, barely. This from the woman who was trembling and hiding under the back steps a little over an hour ago.

Denial is not a river in Egypt.

But I let the subject drop. It wasn't my place to probe into her mental health problems.

We ordered our food and chatted while waiting for it. Rainey was a good conversationalist and she'd led an interesting life. But she tended to talk loudly and gesture a bit flamboyantly at times.

I found myself glancing at the other diners on the patio, some of whom seemed to be ignoring us a little too studiously. Heat crept up my cheeks, but fortunately at that moment, our food arrived.

I dug into mine, which turned out to be the best shrimp quesadillas I'd ever had.

Rainey ate a couple of bites of her burrito, then picked up the conversation again. Somehow she wandered into the details about the sexual assault. Not the assault itself, thank God, but the before and after.

I arranged my face into what I hoped was a sympathetic expression. I'd never been assaulted so I could only begin to imagine her feelings.

She was barely eating now, just taking a bite now and then. I glanced longingly at my remaining quesadilla, now growing cold on my plate. I picked up my knife and blindly cut it up while keeping my eyes on Rainey's face and nodding occasionally to show I was listening.

And I was. The story she told was too appalling to ignore. I even forgot to be embarrassed when nearby diners shot her sharp looks.

Rainey paused to take a bite of food and I slipped a shrimp and some tortilla into my own mouth. I chewed slowly, struggling not to moan. Even room temperature, it was delicious.

"I tried to ignore what was happening to me," Rainey said, "but I was getting so little sleep, because of the nightmares and all." She broke eye contact and gazed down at her plate. "I almost killed a man."

I choked a little on the shrimp I was in the process of swallowing. Putting down my fork, I waved at the waitress, pointed to my plate and used my hands to indicate the sides of an invisible box.

She nodded and disappeared inside the restaurant.

"I gave him the wrong medicine. Thank God my supervisor caught it."

The rest of the story was short and not so sweet. Her commanding officer had packed her off back to the States, and she'd received a medical discharge she hadn't wanted.

Again she dropped her gaze to her plate. "Some people don't believe me when I tell them about all this. Or they make excuses for the Army…" Her voice trailed off.

Sadly I believed her and I told her so. I love my country and have all kinds of respect for the leaders of the armed forces who defend it. But military leaders are people and as susceptible to human flaws as the rest of us, including sexism and expediency. I could easily believe that a commanding officer in a combat situation would choose to believe the man over the woman and ship her off, in order to keep things under control. Even if he secretly believed that she had been raped, he'd justify the decision as necessary. He and his troops needed to be focused on the enemy, not on some internal investigation that might divide the soldiers into opposing camps, those who believed the woman and those who believed the man.

It wasn't the morally right train of thought, but I could see how a commanding officer's mind might go there. I wasn't about to say any of that to Rainey though. It might sound like *I* was defending the Army. Which I wasn't. They had let the victim suffer the punishment, and the perpetrator of the crime had gotten off scot-free.

"At least the medical discharge made it easier to get disability benefits," she was saying. "I tried working at the local hospital when I first got back, but I was a wreck."

She changed the subject back to Lacy and the training, as the waitress arrived with a plastic box and a bag.

I boxed up my food and answered her questions.

Then she excused herself to go to the ladies' room. While she was gone, the waitress brought the check.

Lunch had been her idea so I slid the black faux leather folder over next to her plate.

She didn't bat an eye when she returned to the table. "So glad we had this chance to become besties," she said, as she signed the credit card slip.

Besties? That made me a tad uncomfortable. But I let it slide, knowing our relationship would end in a few weeks when her training was completed.

She hooked her arm through mine as we strolled back toward my car, which made me *more* than a tad uncomfortable. But I didn't pull away.

I had to fight the urge to look around, to see if anyone was watching this way-too-public display of affection.

She must have sensed my discomfort. She dropped her arm to her side. "You worried about people thinking you're a lesbian?"

I almost stopped in my tracks. How did one answer such a question?

I opted for a simple, "No."

Suddenly, Rainey stopped in *her* tracks, her eyes wide, her mouth a small o.

I stopped walking. My head swiveled around, trying to locate whatever had caused such a reaction. I looked back at Rainey.

She was staring at my car–my brand new SUV wannabe that had replaced the sedan I'd totaled a few weeks ago. It now had a jagged scratch in the pale blue paint, all along the passenger side.

Someone had keyed my car.

CHAPTER THREE

"You didn't tell me your car getting keyed had to do with some stalker," Will said.

"I didn't think it did at the time." Anger surged in my chest all over again at the thought that someone had defiled my new baby. It was the first new car I'd bought solely on my own. I vowed to have the side repainted as soon as I got paid for training Lacy.

"And now?" Will asked.

"Now I'm not so sure."

~~~

I'd tried to reassure Rainey as I drove back to her house. "It's just a coincidence."

She kept insisting it had to be her stalker, that he was following her. She begged me to leave Lacy with her for the night.

No way, José, as my mother would say. Lacy hardly knew her and there was a lot Rainey needed to learn before she'd be ready to partner with a service dog.

These dogs aren't watch dogs. Indeed, their natural territorial tendencies are stifled a good bit during the training. They need to stay calm and focused on their handlers when they encounter strangers out in public. And even at home, they can't be barking their heads off whenever the doorbell rings or a squirrel runs by the front window. PTSD sufferers are often sensitive to sudden, loud noises.

"I can't do that," I told her. "You need at least two weeks of training before I can leave Lacy with you."

She turned in the passenger seat to face me, her eyes haunted. "Why?"

I wasn't sure how to respond to that. The answer was because an untrained handler could ruin a well-trained dog, or at least undo some of their training. And I wouldn't get any extra payment for the time it would take to fix that damage.

"It's one of Mattie's rules."

Sorry, Mattie.

I'd barely pulled the car to a stop in front of Rainey's house when she undid her seatbelt and jumped out. She stomped up the walk.

"Okay, that went well," I muttered to myself. Childlike innocence was losing its appeal.

I gave her a few minutes while I got Lacy out of the car and strolled toward the backyard. I was now officially in a bad mood, thanks to the key job on my car and Rainey's antics.

When she didn't come back out of the house, I called her cell number.

"What?" she snapped into the phone.

"You need to come out so we can do this," I said in a firm voice. "If I take this dog home now, I'm going to tell Mattie you're not ready for a service dog."

Actually, I was going to tell Mattie this woman was too unstable, which would be hard to explain, since by definition our clients are less than mentally stable. But a client who's too volatile could become abusive, and one who wasn't willing to take on the responsibilities of caring properly for a dog, that was a deal breaker too.

"Why are you yelling at me?" Rainey sounded like she was about to cry.

I stifled a sigh. "I'm not yelling. I'm just telling you like it is."

Rainey came out, but she was surly for the rest of the afternoon. I got monosyllabic answers most of the time, and her face was unreadable. My guess was she'd gone into military mode and I was her drill sergeant.

So be it, if that got us through this. I didn't want to tell Mattie on her. One, she needed this dog, and two, I needed my training fee, which wouldn't be forthcoming until the dog was permanently in the hands of a client.

When I called it a day and Lacy and I were headed for the gate, Rainey trotted along on the opposite side from the dog. "Please, let her stay tonight."

I clenched my jaw and stopped moving. "I already told you, I can't do that."

"I thought you liked me."

"I do like you," although the truth of that was debatable at that moment, "but I have to follow the rules or I'll lose my job."

Actually, I'm an independent contractor, but trying to explain that right then would've only confused the issue.

"We'll keep at this and you'll be able to have her with you full-time soon. See you tomorrow."

~~~

"So you were leading me on then," Will's deep voice had a chuckle in it, "about coming down here and keeping me occupied."

I let out a dramatic sigh of my own. "Yeah, sorry. I've gotta go up to Ocala this afternoon. How about tonight?"

"Can't. County commissioners' meeting."

"Didn't you just have one of them last week?"

"Yeah, they called an emergency meeting."

"Why?"

"Got me. One of them probably caught somebody jaywalking on Main Street again. Who knows what crazy ordinances they'll pass if I'm not there to point out what is and is not enforceable."

"Well, I guess I'll see you again some time." I winced a little at the slight whine in my voice.

"Maybe Friday evening?"

"Can you come here?" I said. "I've got to be up early Saturday and go to Ocala again."

Yet another sigh. "I can take you to dinner but I should come back to Collinsville afterwards. The new dispatcher's on duty that night, and she's still getting used to the department. I probably shouldn't be too far away, in case there's an emergency."

Mild guilt feelings helped me stifle the urge to push the issue. He'd lost a deputy and a staff person in a mess a few weeks ago, and although I wasn't responsible for what had happened, I'd played a part in bringing it all to a head.

"Okay," I said. "I guess we'll have to see how the week goes."

"Yeah."

"Miss you."

"Miss you too." At least he sounded wistful about it.

We signed off, and I blew out air.

Buddy looked up at me and tilted his head.

I leaned down and scratched behind his ears. "*One* of these days, I'm going to get laid," I told him with more confidence than I felt.

The next couple of days went a bit smoother. I saw little of the sister, and Rainey stayed on task, with the occasional reminder that the sooner we got to a certain point in the training, the sooner Lacy could stay with her full-time.

I packed a PBJ each day for my lunch, to forestall any repeat luncheon invitations. Rainey called me *girlfriend* a couple of times, but I let that slide.

I tried to get her to talk about the stalker, to find out his name, but she would immediately change the subject. If I pushed, she became agitated and defensive. Since I was more invested in getting this training over with than in helping the Marion County Sheriff's Department catch her stalker, I let it go.

But she did talk a lot about old boyfriends from high school and college, so I was pretty sure she was straight. Although she could be bisexual, since she talked a lot about her friend Carrie as well. Actually, she talked a lot in general, especially when she was wound up.

I concluded that she was a very needy person who tended to glom onto people too fast and too hard. Which of course, had the opposite effect from the one she desired. People felt suffocated and pushed her away.

I was trying not to do that. She'd already been damaged enough by the events in her life. I didn't want to add to her neuroses.

When I called it a day on Wednesday, Rainey walked me and Lacy to the gate. I braced myself and told her that I would be back tomorrow but Friday I would need to take a break from our training.

"Why?" she whined.

"I've got a fairly new dog at home. I've been doing short sessions with her in the mornings, before coming up here to Ocala. But I really need to spend a whole day with her and get her back on track. She's starting to backslide."

"But I need Lacy with me. I get so scared after you leave, and at night… It's just awful." She actually stuck out her lower lip. "You say she can't stay until we've gotten through so much of the training, but now you're delaying that?"

"Rainey, I don't usually train with new handlers day in and day out. We train for a few days, then take a break. Gives you a chance to catch your breath and me a chance to take care of other things in my life."

Sunny had walked up during the end of this speech. "Sis, let it go. Marcia has a right to have a life."

I gave Sunny a small smile. "I'll see you all tomorrow."

I pushed through the gate, Lacy trotting at my side. Halfway across the front yard, my cell phone rang. I took it out and smiled at my best friend's name on the caller ID.

"Hey Becky, what's up?" I said in a cheerful voice, grateful to be talking to someone with whom I didn't have to try so hard.

"Hey yourself. What are you up to tonight?"

"Not much. I'm actually in Ocala but headed home now."

"You want to grab some dinner first?"

"Sounds great. Where do you want to meet?"

After some back and forth while I was hooking Lacy to her

safety strap in the backseat, we decided on a Cuban place in Belleview, on the southern side of Ocala. I signed off and backed out of the backseat.

When I straightened up, Rainey was still standing in her yard, looking like a lost child.

"I thought I was your friend." Her voice shook a little.

Sheez!

Out loud, I said, "This isn't about being friends or whether or not I like you. I can't leave Lacy with you until you're sufficiently trained. Not if I want to keep my job."

She stood up straighter, squared the shoulders that had been sagging a moment before. "What if something happens to me," her tone was now semi-belligerent, "before you've deemed it okay for Lacy to stay with me?"

I was at a loss. What did I say to that? As I'd already explained several times, Lacy was not a guard dog.

"Well, let's pray that doesn't happen." Okay, that was lame, but I wasn't sure I cared at this point.

I got in my car and made my escape.

Becky's a massage therapist and she always smelled of something plus shea butter. Tonight it was lavender. Which went well with her outfit, a cotton sundress with small purple and yellow flowers all over it. Its snug top and flowing skirt flattered her near-perfect figure and shapely legs. Her pedicured feet were show-cased in strappy yellow sandals.

I suppressed my usual spurt of envy and self-consciously tugged the hem of my camp shirt down around my ample hips.

The hostess glanced at Lacy but made no comment as she led us to a table. Becky and I ate here fairly often so the staff was used to my bringing along a canine companion in a service dog vest. Indeed, it was one of my favorite spots to take dogs in training to test their ability to resist distractions.

We settled into a booth and Lacy lay down at my feet.

Our food came quickly, despite the fact that the place was

filling up. I dove in. It had been a long time since my peanut butter and jelly lunch.

Par for the course, the waitress wandered over when we both had our mouths full. In heavily accented English, she said, "Chu need anyting else?"

Becky, her mouth full of black bean soup, shook her head, dark curls bouncing against fair cheeks.

"It's delicious," I said around a mouthful of Cuban sandwich.

Becky nodded and rolled her eyes in pleasure.

The waitress flashed us a smile and disappeared.

Cuban sandwiches are popular in Florida, but the ones most sandwich shops and delis serve are bland imitations of the real thing, served by real Cubans–fresh roasted pork and tender ham, Swiss cheese, sharp dill pickles, and a creamy mustard on warm, crusty Cuban bread.

I gobbled down about a quarter of my sandwich before coming up for air.

Becky finished her soup and started on her salad. "So what's up with you? You don't look all that happy tonight. Something happen with Sheriff Will?"

"Ha! I wish it had. That's the problem."

I was really preoccupied with Rainey's on-again, off-again strange behavior, but I wasn't supposed to talk about clients' issues. Might as well focus on my celibate love life instead.

Will and I had been dating for weeks, but we couldn't seem to get certain things in sync. First I'd been skittish, thanks to a marriage that had failed miserably.

He'd been married before as well, but it didn't seem to have left the same kind of scar tissue. His was a different wound–he'd lost contact with his ex-wife's son whom he'd loved as his own.

Sparks exploded all over my body whenever the good sheriff touched me, so lust had eventually trumped my fears, for the most part. But then we'd had a series of inconvenient events get in the way.

Every time we got together, he would get an emergency call

and would have to rush back to Collinsville to deal with some-thing. Once it was a missing child, who was found safe and sound, thank God. Another time a drunken husband had barricaded him-self in his house and threatened to kill his wife and kids.

Will had been able to defuse the situation, but not until it was way too late at night for him to drive back to my house to defuse me!

I live in a tiny town in central Florida called Mayfair, with less than three hundred souls in residence. Its cheap real estate had been all I could afford when I'd moved down here from Maryland a little over two years ago. I'd come to love my little house and the town, but I was two hours away from Will.

"Does he always have to be on call?" Becky asked. "Can't he get a deputy to take over now and again?"

"Not until he gets the new one he recently hired broken in. He's hoping things will ease up in another week or two."

Her eyes went wide. "He expects you to just wait?"

She would never put up with a chaste relationship for half the time I had already. Becky likes her men hot and uninterested in commitment.

"Well, no, we'll get together when we can, but there's no guar-antee that we'll, you know, *really* get together."

She grinned at me. "I hope, after all this anticipation, he's worth it." She'd raised her voice to be heard over the hubbub of the crowded restaurant.

Heat crept up my cheeks. My mind's eye visualized his buff body filling out his khaki uniform. My own body tingled. "Oh, I suspect he will be."

The waitress came by again, carrying a pitcher of iced tea. "Chu like more sweet tea?"

Becky nodded, but I shook my head. On the subject of sweet tea, I'm a staunch Northerner.

The waitress had tilted her pitcher to top off Becky's glass when someone bumped her from behind, shoving her forward. One arm flew up as she struggled not to fall into Becky's lap. The pitcher tipped too far, and tea liberally watered the purple flowers on Becky's dress.

The waitress jumped back. "*¡Aie, lo siento mucho!* I so sorry!"

Becky waved her hand around. "*Nada,*" she managed to get out in a strained voice, her expression attesting to the iced part of the iced tea.

She wiggled out of our booth and headed for the restrooms in the back of the restaurant.

I grabbed both our purses. "Don't take our food," I said to the waitress who was still spluttering apologies. Lacy and I followed the trail of iced tea that led to the tiny ladies' room.

Becky and I used paper towels to sop up the worst of the liquid from her dress, and Becky being Becky, she started laughing. "Well, that's a novel way for tea to make you more alert."

When we got back to the table, the waitress had cleaned up the mess and there were two fresh glasses of iced tea awaiting us next to our plates.

I appreciated the thought behind the gesture but suspected she had forgotten that mine was unsweetened. I took a tentative sip and cringed at the super sweet taste. Yup, she'd forgotten.

Ignoring the drink, I dug into my sandwich again while Becky told me about a new massage technique she'd learned at a recent workshop.

"I haven't tried it out yet. Can I use you as a guinea pig?"

"Sure." I was always up for a free massage. "How about Saturday, late afternoon? I'll need something after finishing up with my client that day."

Becky's eyebrows arched. "Oh? What's going on with this client?"

I shook my head and changed the subject.

The next morning, I had a short session with Jenny out in the backyard. She wasn't quite as "new" as I'd implied to Rainey, but if I neglected her for too long, she would definitely backslide.

She was a gorgeous dog, a golden retriever mixed with some

other breed that lent a more reddish hue to her coat. I was struggling not to fall in love with her.

After an hour, we came inside for a break. My phone was on the counter, plugged in to charge. It beeped, announcing that I had a text message.

It was from Becky. *Did u get my voicemail?*

No. What's up? I texted back.

Call me.

I did and was shocked when I heard Becky's croaking voice. "Hello."

"What's the matter?"

"I think I've got food poisoning."

I'd been there. It was not pretty. "How long have you been sick?"

I signaled for Jenny to go into her crate, then glanced at hers and Lacy's water bowls. They were still full.

"Woke up in the middle of the night," Becky said.

"Have you been drinking water?"

"Can't keep it down."

"I'm on my way. Stay on the line with me."

It scared the crap out of me when she didn't protest. I gestured for Buddy to follow me and grabbed my purse.

CHAPTER FOUR

I made it to Becky's place in record time. I had a key and let myself in, Buddy at my side.

The studio apartment, which had been her landlord's over-sized garage in another lifetime, was empty. "Beck?"

A toilet flushing solved the riddle. Becky stumbled out of the tiny bathroom. Her face was as white as her silk robe.

"Oh, thank God,. She dropped onto the bed and covered her eyes.

I sat on the side of the bed and pinched the back of her hand.

"Ow." But she didn't pull away. She looked exhausted, dark circles like bruises under her eyes.

The little tent of dry skin on her hand was slow to smooth out. "You're dehydrated."

"Not surprised. I've been puking my brains out. Musta been something from the restaurant last night. You feel okay?"

"Yes, I'm fine. Did anything taste off?"

She shook her head slightly, then moaned.

I went to her fridge and got out a bottle of water.

She waved it away. "I'll only throw it up."

"Drink!" I ordered and held the opened bottle to her lips.

She took a few sips, some dribbling down her cheeks.

I got up and went to the corner that was her kitchen. Buddy stayed on the bedside rug but his worried eyes followed me. He knew something was wrong.

I rooted in Becky's dollhouse-sized cabinets. Locating a box of crackers, I brought it back to the bed. "Here. Nibble on one of these."

She groaned softly without opening her eyes. I put a multi-grain, gluten-free cracker in her hand.

After a moment, she lifted it to her lips and nibbled her way through half of it. I held the water bottle to her lips again. She drank a couple of sips.

I glanced at my watch. I was due at Rainey's in less than an hour. I dug out my phone and called her house.

"Hello?" Sunny's voice, unusually tentative.

"Hey, Sunny. This is Marcia. Are you okay?"

"Yeah. But we just got a bunch of hang-ups in a row. It's got Rainey kind of freaked out. Me too, for that matter."

"No wonder. I would be." I hesitated. "I'm sorry to sound insensitive to what you all are going through with this stalker. But a close friend of mine is really sick. I need to stay with her today. Could you tell Rainey I'll be there on Saturday?"

"Sure, sure, I'll tell her. And Marcia, it's not your responsibility to help my sister deal with this guy." Her voice was firm, almost angry. "Rainey has a tendency to expect too much of people, so don't let yourself get sucked into that."

I held the phone slightly away from my ear and stared at it for a second. Perhaps I hadn't been giving Sunny enough credit.

"Uh, thanks for saying that. Tell Rainey I am truly sorry that I can't come today."

Becky had finished her cracker. She held out her hand for another. I gave it to her, then held the water bottle up. She took it with her other hand and sipped from it, then ate the cracker.

"Marcia, you're a lifesaver."

Becky was still weak at nine that night. Twice, I'd considered taking her to the ER.

Her larder and fridge contained mostly yogurt, tofu and organic nuts, none of which struck me as easy to digest. Well, maybe the tofu, but I had no idea how to prepare it. So I'd fed her more crackers and plied her with water.

Buddy had lain by her bed, that worried look in his eyes. Periodically he sat up and plopped his big black head onto the side of the mattress. Becky gave him a feeble pat or two. Then I motioned for him to lie down again.

I'd called my neighbor's daughter to let Lacy and Jenny out midday. Lacy knew Sybil, but her coming into the house would be a disruption for Jenny. It might set her back in her training, but it couldn't be helped.

I called Sybil again at nine-thirty and asked her to take them out in the backyard for another bathroom break, then feed and crate them for the night.

At eleven, Becky insisted I go home. "I feel much better now. No clients tomorrow morning, so I can rest and recuperate. You need to get back to your dogs."

She was feisty enough to shoot down my protests, so I figured she was truly on the mend.

Buddy and I headed home.

The next day was my official day off from Rainey Bryant. I slept in a whole half hour past my normal wake-up time. I texted Becky to check on her, then took Buddy for a walk.

As usual, strolling through town relaxed me. Mayfair was a ghost town on the rebound. It had been the home of a now defunct, tourist-trap alligator farm and had died back to less than fifty residents. Then telecommuting geeks, retirees and Northern transplants like myself started arriving, breathing life back into it.

Ironically, the folks I was closest to in town were not the thirty-something geeks nor the young couples lured here by dirt-cheap real estate. They were two of the long-term residents, Edna Mayfair, the elderly sister of the now-deceased Mr. Mayfair who had owned the alligator farm and founded the town, and Sherie Wells, the reigning matriarch of the African-American family that had lived here since the sixties. Her father-in-law had worked for Mr. Mayfair, overseeing the maintenance of the alligator farm as well as the old man's mansion—now occupied by one of the telecommuting geeks.

My sleeping in meant that I'd almost missed Edna as she walked her two Springer Spaniels, Benny and Bo. I caught sight of them heading back toward the Mayfair Motel. The black and white dogs, physically grown but still puppies mentally at eighteen months, jumped and twisted on the ends of their leashes.

Edna pulled on their leashes and told them to hush, with no visible impact on their behavior. Buddy was "off duty," so I unhooked the leash from his collar. It would just get tangled up with theirs. He romped ahead on the sidewalk to sniff butts.

"Good mornin', Marcia," Edna called out. Today's attire consisted of a muumuu covered in orchids in various shades of purple, and it must be spring indeed because Edna had turned in her winter footwear, lined moccasins, for flip flops.

"Can't linger," she said as I approached. She gestured in the direction of the motel. "Got guests checkin' in later." She was huffing a little.

A frisson of worry moved through me. The woman was in her eighties. Was her health starting to give out on her? I leaned down to hide my concerned expression and patted each of "the boys" on the head. "How're you doing, Edna?"

She waved a hand in the air, as if my question were a pesky mosquito. "Hey, did I tell ya that Dexter's goin' back to school? He got into that trade school up in Ocala." For the next ten minutes, Edna regaled me with the new career options her great nephew would have after completing a two-year course of study.

She finally ran down. "Well, I better skedaddle if I'm gonna get them rooms cleaned in time."

"Tell Dexter I said best of luck." I sketched her a wave as she dragged "the boys" away from Buddy and hurried toward the motel.

I hurried a little myself, heading back to my house, anxious to get in some quality training time with Jenny.

But I wasn't finished with the small-town round of polite visits just yet. Sherie Wells stepped out onto her porch as I walked up the sidewalk to my front door. She was a tall, sixtyish woman with ramrod-straight posture that always made whatever she wore look sophisticated. Today it was black slacks and a white, short-sleeved knit top. "Mornin', Marcia."

"Good morning, ma'am." Despite the fact that she called me Marcia, I'd yet to get up the nerve to call Mrs. Wells by her first name.

She swiped back a tendril of black and silver hair that had escaped from the chignon on the back of her head. "Haven't seen a lot of you lately."

"I've been working with a client, Lacy's new owner."

The corners of her mouth turned down. "Aw, so that sweet pup won't be around much longer."

I ignored the ache in my chest. "Sadly, no. That's the big downside of doing this for a living, having to let go of the dogs when they graduate from training."

"Hey, we might be getting a new neighbor." Mrs. Wells gestured toward the curb in front of my house. "There was a car parked out there for a good while yesterday."

The Wells house and mine were the only occupied buildings on this end of Main Street. Most of the other cottages that had once made up the black section of town were now rotting shells overgrown with weeds and palmettos. There would be no reason for someone to park so far from the rest of the town unless they were visiting me or the Wells clan. But the cottage on the other side of me was still in relatively good shape, and a for-sale sign had adorned its front yard for the whole time I'd lived next door.

Mrs. Wells wrinkled her nose. "The car was old, kind of banged up. A green sedan."

"Then it might very well be somebody looking at that house. I suspect the owners would take any offer at this point."

She sniffed. "Well, I hope it's somebody nice like you and not some trashy folks."

I grinned at her. The vehicle I'd arrived in two and a half years ago had been old and banged up as well. "Me too. And thanks for the compliment."

Once inside my house, I let Buddy lap up some water. Then he and Jenny and I went out back.

My yard was perfect for training animals. It wasn't much wider than the house but it was long, and a previous owner had erected a six-foot, wooden privacy fence. At the far end was a stand of palm trees and Southern pines that blocked the worst of the glare from the morning sun. And right in the middle of the yard was a big old magnolia tree. In another month or two, its glossy green leaves would be interspersed with gorgeous white blooms.

While Buddy snoozed under that tree, I went through the basic signals that Jenny already knew. She was so smart and eager to please. I could feel her pulling on my heartstrings. Yet another one I'd have trouble letting go of when the time came.

Since I wouldn't be able to spend much time with her over the next few days, I wasn't going to introduce anything new, but reinforcement of prior learning was always a good thing. We reviewed the nose touch and the cover command–she was a little sketchy on that one, although she did it three times out of four.

I walked over to the magnolia tree and halted just outside the circle of shade. Jenny stopped dutifully beside me, and turned to face back the way we'd come.

Excellent.

I called Buddy's name, and when I had his attention I twirled my finger around in a circle. It was a signal I'd devised for him that meant he was to run around and act like somebody's pet, trying to get Jenny to play with him.

He jumped up and woofed, then trotted over and sniffed Jenny's butt.

She looked up at me, a touch of confusion in her eyes. I held out my hand and she touched the palm with her nose. Then she went back to staring behind me, "covering my back." She ignored Buddy as he romped around, barking and wagging his tail like crazy.

It's important that service dogs be resistant to distractions, and the greatest distraction is another dog. I would test her eventually with Edna's enthusiastic pups, but for now Jenny was doing great.

I waved my hand in the signal for Buddy to stop. He cut off in mid bark and trotted back to the shade under the magnolia.

"Good girl," I praised Jenny.

I gave her the release signal, arms crossed at the wrists, then opened wide, then crossed again–a gesture picked intentionally because it was unlikely anyone would make it by accident. Then I rubbed her head and scratched behind her ears. "You are such a good girl," I cooed.

Her golden-red tail waved in the air like a flag.

We broke for lunch, then ran through the whole repertoire of signals again. Jenny was responding faster and surer each time.

I was well pleased.

That was, until I pulled my silenced phone out of my pocket and checked for messages.

Tied up down here. Can't do dinner. Miss u. Will

The next morning I awoke with a feeling of dread in my stomach. Usually I enjoy working with the veterans almost as much as I do with the dogs. I have a masters degree in counseling psychology and being able to apply it to help my clients adjust to their new service animals is gratifying.

But Rainey was a whole different story. I couldn't quite figure out what made her tick.

I was munching my way through my breakfast cereal when a loud knock on the front door set Jenny off. Buddy and Lacy knew better.

That needs more work, I thought as I walked through the living room. "Quiet." I held out my hand and made the down motion.

Jenny quieted and dropped to her belly in her crate.

At the door, Charlene, Mayfair's sole postal worker, handed me a corrugated cardboard carton, slightly larger than a shoebox. "Sorry to bother you, Marcia, but this wouldn't fit in your mailbox."

"No problem. Thanks." The box was very light.

She touched the brim of her USPS baseball cap. "Happy to serve."

I watched her back as she returned to her truck, a vague sense of guilt compressing my chest. Rainey Bryant had been happy to serve her country, and here I was dreading spending the day with her to train her how to partner with her dog. A service dog she wouldn't need if she hadn't been happy to serve her country.

I examined the box as I returned to my half-soggy bran flakes. My name and address were written in block letters, with no return address.

I love getting packages, even if it's only the vitamins I order online. I get a little jolt of excitement, like I'm five again and it's Christmas morning.

While I finished my breakfast, I stared at the box, letting the anticipation build. Then I got out scissors and cut the tape holding the flaps closed. The packing inside was crumpled sheets of white paper, rough, and in places, stiff and stained a light tan.

Had whatever was in the box leaked? I was wracking my brain. Had I ordered anything recently? Dog shampoo maybe?

I rooted through the packing material, expecting to find a bottle of brown liquid somewhere in its folds. But there was nothing else in the box. I pulled all the paper out and dumped the box upside down. Nothing.

As I stuffed the crumpled papers back inside, I tried to figure out what this meant. The pieces of paper looked vaguely familiar.

I picked up the next to the last piece and a smear of blue caught my eye. I turned it over. Writing on the other side, again in block letters.

STAY AWAY FROM OCALA.

I sat down hard in a kitchen chair, staring at one stiff, stained corner of the note.

A lightbulb went off. The papers in the box weren't for packing. They were paper towels, *used* paper towels. And the dried stains were the reddish-brown liquid they'd soaked up.

They were the paper towels Becky and I had used on her iced tea-drenched dress.

Bran-flavored bile rose in the back of my throat. What kind of sicko wraps up used paper towels and sends them to people?

CHAPTER FIVE

My shaking hand struggled to get the phone out of the pocket of my jeans. I punched a speed dial number.

"Sheriff Haines."

I told Will about the box and its contents, hating the tremor in my voice. "What do you think it means?"

"I don't know, but I'd prefer you stay away from that woman you've been training with. At least, until I can get the box and paper towels analyzed."

"You think this is related to her stalker?"

"Don't know, but this stuff started happening to you after you began working with her."

My mind flashed back to leaving the restaurant Monday at lunchtime. I reminded Will about Rainey linking arms with me. "Maybe my client's bisexual, or the stalker thinks she might be."

"And he now sees you as competition. You gotta stay away from her, until I can figure out who this is."

I blew out air. "I can't. She's already freaking out about not having Lacy with her at night. If I tell her we have to delay the training, she'll go ballistic. And if she complains to Mattie, who knows what her reaction will be."

"Then I'm going with you, at least for today and tomorrow."

"I can't ask you to do that. Surely you have things you planned to do this weekend."

His voice dropped. "Nothing that's more important than you."

Despite the gravity of the situation, my body warmed and

my chest filled with little bubbles of joy. How could any woman resist those words coming from her man?

I almost let three little words of my own slip out, one of them starting with L. Horrified at myself, I gulped and then cleared my throat.

"Be honest, Marcia," Will said. "You'd feel better if I went."

"Has anybody ever told you that you're a very sweet man?"

A low chuckle. "Yeah, the people I arrest tell me that all the time. I'll be there by noon."

Hopefully no emergency would drag him back to Collinsville before the training session was done, and maybe, just maybe I could convince him to spend the night.

But first we had to get through the day.

I called Rainey's house to tell her I would be running late. I was not looking forward to her reaction. But I lucked out. Sunny picked up the phone.

She took my vague "something's come up" explanation on face value. "Okay, I'll tell Sis. Drive safe."

Will arrived, looking way too sexy in jeans and a short-sleeved chambray shirt. He insisted we take his car, since the stalker wouldn't recognize it. I transferred Lacy's safety strap to his backseat and we started for Ocala.

"Hope this guy doesn't key your car," I said.

"Well, if he does the county commissioners will be told that I do not know exactly where nor when said damage occurred to county property."

I snickered in spite of the subject of conversation. "You sound like a police report."

"Exactly." He flashed me a grin. "That's what'll go in my report."

"So this isn't your car?"

"Nope, provided by Collins County."

"What about the police cruiser you sometimes drive?"

"Just one of our extensive fleet of five patrol cars and a

motorcycle."

Surprised, I asked, "Do you ride motorcycles?"

"Nope. Nobody in the department rides them anymore."

"Why not sell the bike then?"

"I tried. The commissioners wouldn't let me."

"Boy, they really are flaky."

He snorted. "That's a kind way of saying it."

The drive to Rainey's went by much faster than it did when I made it alone. It felt good to have Will's company.

Way too good, the still gun-shy part of me said.

We turned onto Rainey's street. "Um, I think we'll leave out the part that you're a law enforcement officer. I'll just say that you had business up this way so you dropped me off."

"I was planning on sticking around and watching the house."

My conscience insisted that I selflessly ask, "What about the whole being-too-far-away-from-Collinsville thing?"

"I've got pretty good coverage today. It should be fine."

I breathed out pent-up air. That crazy delivery this morning had rattled me more than I cared to admit. "Can you do your surveillance from further down the street?" I was a bit worried about Sunny's reaction.

"Yeah, that might be better even. Maybe lull this guy into trying something so I can catch him at it."

Will stopped three houses short of Rainey's. While I retrieved Lacy from the backseat, he popped his trunk and rummaged in its depths. He came up with a bucket, a bag of corn chips, and a bottle of water. He held up the items. "Emergency surveillance kit."

"I'm sorry you're stuck with spending a boring Saturday watching a street and a bunch of houses."

He shrugged. "Not the first time. Keep your eyes and ears open. If anything weird happens, call me."

"Got it." I walked toward the house, Lacy trotting beside me.

Rainey was standing on her front porch, arms crossed over her chest. "Well, it's about time."

The snarky part of me, which is often about three-quarters

of me, wanted to say, *Well, good afternoon to you, too.* But for once I reined in my tongue. I just wanted to get this training process done.

She was back to treating me like her drill sergeant, complete with the occasional, exaggerated "Yes, ma'am," or "No, ma'am." She even gave me a mock salute one time when my instructions came out sharper than I'd intended.

But after about an hour and a half, she started to loosen up. During a short break, she even asked me how my friend Becky was doing. "I was sorry to hear that she was sick." Her voice was neutral, just being polite really, but I appreciated the effort.

"Hold out your hand," I said. She did and I dropped a handful of treats into her palm. "The training is never really done. You'll need to reinforce Lacy's skills periodically with short training sessions back here, away from distractions. So let's put her through her paces again, and you give her treats when she does what's expected."

Rainey moved to hand Lacy a treat.

"Nope. Don't give treats any other time. Only when the dog is working. Walk across the lawn and stop now and then. She'll go into the cover position. Don't give her a treat then. Wait until you start moving and then give her one. And don't give her a treat every time, only some of the time. That way she won't always expect a reward."

"Intermittent reinforcement." Rainey produced her first smile of the day. "I remember studying that in psychology class in college."

I returned the smile. "Exactly."

The first time she offered a treat, Lacy looked at me for permission. I nodded. "It's okay, girl."

We kept working for another hour. I replenished Rainey's supply of treats. A few minutes later, I called for a second break. Lacy's tongue was hanging out.

"Give her the release signal."

Lips pressed into a grim line, Rainey crossed her wrists rather awkwardly, then pulled them apart. She forgot to cross them again.

It wasn't the first time she had seemed uncomfortable with the release signal.

Lacy looked at me. I repeated the signal, then leaned down and removed the red service dog vest. Lacy shook herself.

As we strolled toward the house, I said, "What's going on when you release her?"

Rainey stopped walking and gave me a wide-eyed look.

I stopped too. Lacy's gaze shifted back and forth between us, no doubt wondering why we were still outside in the hot sun.

"The off-duty signal," I said, "is it triggering something?"

PTSD creates a field of emotional land mines in the sufferer's mind. Explosions of anxiety could be set off by the most commonplace things, like a certain gesture or the whir of a ceiling fan, things that were somehow associated with the trauma the person had experienced.

Rainey bit her lower lip. Her eyes pooled with tears. "The guy, the soldier who…"

Lightbulb moment. "He tied you up," I said gently.

Face pinched, she nodded.

"Then how could they think it was consensual?" The question was out of my mouth before I'd thought it through.

And she took it the wrong way. "It *wasn't* consensual."

"No, no." I softened my voice. "I know it wasn't. I'm just that much more shocked that they didn't believe you."

She looked away, toward the porch a couple of dozen feet in front of us. "He said it was S and M foreplay, and that I'd asked to do that."

My stomach lurched. "I'm so sorry you went through that."

She nodded, her head still turned away.

"This guy who's been stalking you, did you date him since you got out of the Army?"

She nodded again, finally met my gaze. "I, uh, didn't want to have sex as often as he did, because of…" She swung her arm in a vague gesture. "So he broke up with me. But then he kept calling and writing, and then doing weird stuff, threatening things, like that paint on the wall."

Ironically, she sounded less and less upset the longer she talked about her stalker. Even he was a preferable topic over the man who'd assaulted her.

"What's your ex-boyfriend's name?"

She shook her head.

But now that she was talking about the guy, I wasn't about to give up. "Rainey, I didn't tell you this before because I didn't want to freak you out, but some other things have happened. I think this guy's also fixated on me now."

"Gawd, he's like the ebola virus, spreading to anybody I come into contact with. He's done some stuff to my sister as well. And my friend Carrie."

"Like what?"

"Anonymous notes, among other things, telling them to butt out."

"He assumed they were trying to keep you apart."

"Yeah, which makes no sense." She dropped her gaze to the ground next to my feet. "He broke up with me initially. I just refused to take him back. Carrie did have something to do with that. She convinced me he would just hurt me again."

"Look, I really need to know his name, and a better description. Right now, this guy could walk up to me, give me his real name, and tell me he was selling magazine subscriptions, and I wouldn't even know he was dangerous."

She raised her head. Her face was pale. "Come on. I think I still have a picture of him."

Inside, we headed toward the stairs leading to her attic bedroom, Lacy trailing along. I dropped the package of treats I was carrying on the kitchen table.

Rainey's room was most of the attic. A boxy air conditioner rattled away in the window of the dormer on the front of the house. Still the room was warm. Second floors are hard to cool in Florida which is why so many houses here are one-story ranchers.

Rainey ignored the red bull's eye on the other window and headed for a small computer desk in one corner of the room. She rooted through some papers next to her monitor. "Here it is." She handed me a snapshot, then turned back toward the desk.

In the picture, she and the young man were in swimsuits, a beach and rolling waves in the background. They were both smiling, not a care in the world, and he had his arm around her waist.

I glanced over at Rainey. Her head was hanging. Tear stains spread on the papers on the desk.

I found myself once again feeling bad for her.

"I really cared about him," she said without turning around. "I probably would've gotten back together with him, if he hadn't started doing weird crap."

I put a hand on her shoulder and squeezed gently. She covered it with her own hand and squeezed back.

Then she swiped at her eyes with her fingers. "Sorry. I didn't mean to get all weepy. I guess I've been so busy being scared of him lately that I didn't finish getting over the hurt."

It was the most insightful thing I'd ever heard her say. In that moment I realized, had we met under different circumstances, we might very well have become friends.

"Come on. I'm parched. Let's get some tea." She led the way to the kitchen.

Sunny had baked poppy seed muffins for us and, I suspected out of deference to me, had made a pitcher of unsweetened iced tea. I was touched by her thoughtfulness.

She brushed off my thanks. "I can't stand all that sugar either."

We ate warm muffins and drank cool tea. I thought of poor Will, sitting out in his car, and felt a twinge of guilt.

"Um, I think it's time for you to start working with Lacy alone." I held up my hand at Rainey's joyful look. "I'm not leaving her overnight yet, but we need to be working toward that, so I'm going to take a walk."

What Rainey didn't know was that I was ad-libbing, looking for a way to get out of the house and away from their scrutiny for a few minutes.

"You take Lacy out back and work with her some more. Put her through her paces. We'll see how she reacts when I'm not around."

I stood up and leaned toward the plate of muffins. "Mind if I take another one with me?"

"Of course not," Sunny said with a smile.

I poured myself another glass of iced tea as well, adding a little more sugar than I usually use. Scooping up my napkin with one finger, I headed for the front door.

Lacy stood to follow me. "No. Lie down, girl." To Rainey I said, "Once I'm out of the house, put her vest on her and take her out back. She should be fine with you."

Sunny moved around me to open the door.

"Thanks."

I strolled down the front walk and turned left toward the spot further along the block where Will's car was parked. Juggling muffin, napkin and iced tea glass into one hand, I dug my phone out of my pocket and called him.

When he answered, I said in my most sultry voice, "Hey, big boy, what's cookin'?"

"Me," he said. "Don't know what possessed the county commissioners to buy a dark-colored car." Most cars in Florida are white or light colors, to repel as much of the intense sun as possible.

"I've got an iced tea for you, and a delicious muffin. What do I get in return?"

I heard his stomach growl through the phone, and I laughed out loud.

"Hmm, I think we could arrange some appropriate recompense this evening," he said.

I was almost to his car. "Lordy, you're sexy when you use fancy words like *recompense*."

He chuckled. "You can leave those goodies by that bush." Through the slightly tinted windshield, I saw his arm come up, pointing to a big crepe myrtle near his car. "I'll get them after you're back inside."

Instead, I turned abruptly and started back the other way. To the casual observer I was just another young person absorbed with her cell phone.

I exaggerated the swing of my hips as I walked away from him. "Would you care to elaborate on the appropriate recompense?"

"Has anyone ever told you, Ms. Banks, that you are a tease?"

I added a little extra swish of my butt.

He chortled into the phone. "You know, I don't think I've ever had phone sex while doing a stakeout before."

I laughed. "Hey, who's calling who a tease? You're the one who's bolted from my arms the last two times we've gotten together."

"Sorry. Comes with the territory, I'm afraid."

I didn't say anything, since my own vocation put constraints on our love life as well. I couldn't spend the night at his place because of the dogs. The ones in training needed as few distractions and disruptions in their routine as possible.

Not to mention what the Collinsville rumor mill would do with that, and what damage would be done to Will's chances for re-election.

"Do I get the muffin and tea?" he said. "I'm dry as a bone. My water ran out a while ago."

I turned and headed back his way. "Okay, I'll put them under that bush, but there's a hitch. I have to take the glass back in with me."

"I'll pour the tea into my empty water bottle while you walk the other way. Then you can retrieve the glass."

I left the contraband under the bush and walked away again. "All this cloak and dagger is a real turn-on," I said into the phone.

"Gotta put my phone down now to get the stuff."

"Now what kind of response is that?' I said with mock indignation. "You prefer muffins and tea over sexy talk with me?"

"As hungry and thirsty as I am now, in a word, yes."

I chuckled and pretended to still be talking to someone as I walked up the block again, past Rainey's house.

A few minutes went by, then Will said in my ear, "Got 'em. Thanks."

"Okay, I'm going to try to shake loose from here in another hour or so. Hang in there." I disconnected and turned back to retrieve the glass.

The kitchen was empty when I returned to the house. I left the glass on the counter by the sink and went out back.

The rest of the training that afternoon went fairly smoothly. Until Rainey's phone pinged in her pocket just as I was explaining a new command to her.

She immediately hauled the phone out and stared at it. "It's Carrie," she said without looking up. Her thumb darted back and forth across the screen.

I cleared my throat. She didn't react. Or at least not to me.

She smiled at the screen, and her thumb did its little dance again.

"Rainey, I'd appreciate it if you'd turn your phone off while we're training."

She looked at me as if I'd spoken to her in Swahili.

"We need to get back to work. I've got to go soon."

She frowned at me, then down at the screen. Her thumb tapped out one more text before she pocketed the phone.

And I was back to drill sergeant status.

I stifled a sigh.

As I was getting ready to leave an hour later, I told Rainey I would work on a new release signal. "It won't be that hard to substitute a different one. We'll use them both for a while and Lacy will adjust."

She unbent and smiled. Then the next thing I knew she was hugging me. "Thank you. You're the best."

I awkwardly wrapped my arms around her and patted her back.

She bounded up the back porch steps, and I let myself out through the gate.

Once Lacy and I were settled into Will's car and he'd headed for the highway, I leaned my head back against the headrest and closed my eyes. I was having one of my annoying niggling feelings.

After a few minutes, it dawned on me. The package of treats I'd left on Rainey's kitchen table–I'd never retrieved it. Indeed, I didn't remember seeing it there when we sat down to have iced tea and muffins. Had Rainey assumed they were for her and put them away somewhere?

Oh well, it was no big deal. The package was only half full and the treats weren't expensive.

I sighed.

A warm hand patted my thigh. I covered it and squeezed. Then Will withdrew his hand to put it back on the steering wheel.

I would've loved to have taken a short nap, but the niggling feeling hadn't departed. All I could figure out was that it had something to do with Becky. I made a mental note to call her when I got home. Right now, I needed to rest a few minutes.

I was starting to drift off when Will asked, "Did you get the name of the stalker?"

My eyes flew open. *Crapola!*

I sat up in the passenger seat.

I'd gotten Rainey talking about the guy, had even gotten a picture of him, but she'd never actually said his name.

I sheepishly admitted to Will how much I suck as an investigator and repeated the guy's description, handing over the snapshot Rainey had given me.

"I'll get her to tell me his name tomorrow," I said.

He slipped the picture into his shirt pocket and opened his mouth.

The car pitched and rocked to one side, accompanied by an ominous thumping from the rear end.

CHAPTER SIX

My stomach heaved in concert with the sideways roller coaster. "What's going on?" I yelled to be heard over the thumping.

Will was wrestling with the steering wheel. "I think we have a flat tire."

Unfortunately, we were now on I-75, a highway notorious for fast-moving traffic and drivers who believed they were invincible. Either that or they all had a death wish.

Will pulled as far off the road as he could, with half the car on the grass beyond the shoulder. Still, it would be risky business changing a tire on the driver's side. "Wish I were wearing my uniform."

"Why? You think people would slow down then?"

"No but the cop who arrests them after they hit me would know to throw the book at them."

I tried to smile but it really wasn't funny.

"You and Lacy better get out and stand way back, just in case somebody runs into the back of the car."

"Why would they do that?"

"Not paying attention and they think this car is still moving in a traffic lane."

Oh joy!

I got out and quickly undid Lacy from her safety strap in the backseat. We walked about twenty feet into the tall grass, with me praying there was nothing worse than mosquitoes lurking in there. Lacy seemed relaxed enough so I figured we were okay. I jumped when a tiny lizard scuttled across my sneaker.

Keeping one eye on the traffic, Will hurried to change the tire in the gathering dusk. A couple of times, he dropped his tools and darted around one end of the car or the other as a tractor trailer barreled past at full speed in the lane right next to us.

By the time he was done, we were both nervous wrecks. I loaded Lacy back in the car, and we set out again for my house.

Once he'd pulled into the flow of traffic and brought the car up to speed, he glanced my way, a frown creasing his face. "There was a roofing nail in the tire."

"You have any idea where you picked it up?"

He shook his head. "Haven't been near any construction sites recently. I've got a bad feeling about it."

"What do you mean?"

"Best way to give someone a flat tire and throw them off about who did it is to drive a nail in the tire. The leak is slow and they're some distance away by the time it goes all the way flat."

"You think it was the stalker?"

"Maybe, but how'd he connect me to your client?"

I gave a little shrug. "He saw us drive up together?"

"Could be. But you'd think with me watching the house, he'd lay low, not draw attention to himself by doing something to my car."

"But you said people use that technique so the flat tire won't get blamed on them."

"True."

"How could he even get close enough to do that? You were in the car the whole time."

"Almost the whole time. He'd have to be quick." Will was quiet for a moment, staring out the windshield. "It would be doable, if he had the nail and hammer ready, had been watching for his chance."

He shook his head. "It doesn't make any sense. If it's supposed to be another warning to stay away from Rainey Bryant, why make it look like a nail I accidentally picked up along the way?"

"Or," I said, "we're overanalyzing this and it *is* a nail you accidentally picked up along the way."

He gave me a lopsided grin. "Just because you're paranoid and all that."

We rode in silence for a few minutes. "Are you staying over?" I asked.

He glanced my way, one eyebrow arched. "Am I invited?"

"Oh yeah!"

"Okay then, but I was at the hardware store when you called earlier. I didn't take the time to go home and pack my jammies and toothbrush."

"Hmm, I might have a new toothbrush around the house somewhere. My dentist is always giving them to me." I placed my hand lightly on his thigh. "And I don't think you'll need your jammies."

He gave me another eyebrow-arched glance. "You'll wanna be careful where you let that hand wander. This traffic's pretty bad."

I lifted my hand and used my index and middle fingers like legs to walk it down his thigh to his knee, which I patted twice, then removed the hand to my own lap.

His face was quite flushed.

I sat back in my seat and smirked.

Once home, I let the dogs out for a bathroom break while I freshened their water bowls and filled their food dishes with kibble. When I brought the dogs back inside, Lacy immediately lapped up most of the water from her bowl.

"You got quite the workout today, didn't you, girl?" I grabbed the bowl and headed for the kitchen.

"What are we eating?" Will said.

"Good question." Mayfair was a good half hour from any grocery store or restaurant, other than the Mayfair diner, which was only open for breakfast and lunch. "We probably should've stopped for something." I sure as heck didn't feel like going out again.

I returned Lacy's refilled water bowl to her crate, and went back to the kitchen to root in my freezer. I came up with a frozen cheese pizza.

Will grimaced, then nodded.

"Sorry. I do have some decent wine. Becky gave it to me for Christmas. I've been saving it for a special occasion."

Will's face brightened.

"Speaking of whom," I said as I pulled the bottle of wine from a cabinet, "I need to call Becky." I wanted to check on her, but I'd also just remembered my free massage was supposed to have happened this afternoon. That was probably what the nagging feeling had been about.

Will took the bottle from me and set it on the counter, then he hauled me against him and kissed me soundly. My insides melted. Something warm wiggled against my right hip.

Will's hand came up with my phone in it. "Text her. It'll be faster."

I grinned as I took the phone from him. "I won't be long. Stick the pizza in the oven, would you?"

I walked into the living room, phone in hand, texting away. *How r u doing?*

Much better.

Sorry couldn't come for massage. With Will. I hoped she didn't mind being supplanted by a man, but the situation was too complicated to explain in a text.

After a couple of seconds, she responded, *Ride him, cowgirl!*

I laughed and shook my head. *LOL Call u tomorrow.*

Lacy whined a little as she paced back and forth in her crate. I would have thought she'd be tired, after her long day. I gestured for her to lie down. She complied and rested her chin on her paws.

Having finished his dinner, Buddy followed me back into the kitchen.

Will had found plates and napkins in the cabinets and was carrying two wineglasses to the table. "That pizza's going to take a few minutes." He twisted the screw cap off the wine bottle. "Hate to see what Becky considers cheap wine."

He poured the ruby red liquid into the glasses, then handed

one to me.

We clinked glasses and took a sip.

He nodded slightly. "Actually, it's not too bad."

I concurred, but then what did I know about wine. My ex-husband had been a bit of a connoisseur. I'd followed his lead, drinking whatever he handed me.

And now history was repeating itself. Well, sort of. The wine was not as good, but the guy sipping it with me was a lot better.

I smiled at Will. He took my glass away from me, set it and his own on the table and gathered me to him again.

When we broke for air, I murmured, "Hmm, I could get used to this."

"I'm hoping you do," he said, his breath warm against my cheek.

More melting inside. Will's lips found mine again, and my knees went all wobbly. He wrapped an arm firmly around my waist and held me up.

It took a moment for the sound to penetrate my sex-crazed brain. A hacking noise from the living room.

I pulled away from Will and bolted around the corner.

Lacy had exploded from both ends.

CHAPTER SEVEN

Will smacked his palm on his steering wheel. "If only I had one of the cruisers, I could put on lights and siren."

"Collins County bought you a car, but no siren?"

He gave me a quick glance, then eyes forward again as we sped down the road. "We're talking about the county commissioners from hell here, remember?"

"Oh, yeah." I didn't want to know how fast we were going. "That's really the epitome of penny wise and pound foolish though."

Another quick glance. "Is that another motherism?"

I gave him a feeble smile. He was always razing me about the old-fashioned words and sayings I'd picked up from my mother. And his gentle teasing was making inroads into the insecurities bred by the mean boys in middle school, who had not so lovingly made fun of my name and what they'd called my "prissy ways."

Being a pastor's kid is no fun. The parishioners frown at you whenever you slip and say anything stronger than *dang*. And the other kids tease you for being a goody two shoes.

I shook my head at myself. *Goody two shoes… yet another motherism.*

Retching sounds came from the backseat. I cringed. "Sorry about your upholstery."

"What do you think's wrong with her?"

I looked at poor Lacy, panting in the back. Her eyes were glassy. My throat tightened. "I don't know, but this can't be good."

My hand flew to my mouth. "Crapola! I left the oven on."

"I turned it off, and you might want to use a different expletive right now. We have more than enough crap already."

Will spun the wheel, and the car careened into the parking lot of the emergency veterinarian clinic in Belleview.

I jumped out, unhooked the safety strap and gathered Lacy up as best I could in my arms.

"Here, I've got her." Will took the shaking dog from me. "Get the door."

Will held my hand in the waiting area while the vet, Doc Murdock, and his assistant worked on Lacy in an exam room. The staff knew me. I brought my dogs here all the time, although usually during normal business hours for routine things like vaccines.

Lacy had been here just two weeks ago for a complete checkup. She'd been in perfect health.

The clinic had been about to close for the evening when we got there, but Doc's young receptionist, Joy, had stuck around to keep us company.

She brought us two mugs of coffee. Her pert nose wrinkled as she handed them to us.

I self-consciously rubbed at the dried smear of I-didn't-want-to-think-about-it on my tank top. Will had several similar smears on his shirt.

Bless her heart, Joy plastered a big smile on her face.

I took one of the mugs gratefully. "Do you know what's going on in there?"

Joy shook her head. "But you know Doc's the best. She's in good hands."

Doc Murdock emerged from the exam room and walked across the empty waiting area. I jumped up.

"How…" I couldn't get words past the lump in my throat.

Dear God, let her be okay.

Will stood and put an arm around my shoulders.

"Sit," Doc Murdock said, making a gesture similar to my signal to the dogs to lie down.

We obeyed and the vet sat down next to me. He patted my knee. "We've flushed out her system as best we could, and I've got her on an IV to restore her fluids."

"Is she going to be okay?"

"I think so. We'll know more by morning. Marcia, if it was anyone but you, I'd be asking about what that dog has eaten recently. But I know you train your dogs not to eat anything without permission."

"Doctor," Will said, "pretend for a minute that it's not her. What questions would you be asking?"

Doc Murdock looked at me, his eyebrows partway in the air.

"Oh, sorry. This is my, uh, boyfriend, Will Haines. Sheriff Haines, from Collins County."

"Collins County?" Doc said. "Never heard of it."

"It's pretty small," Will said. "Sandwiched between Sumter and Lake counties."

Doc Murdock sat back in the plastic chair, his rotund body making it squeak a little in protest. "Did she act agitated earlier, or lethargic?"

"She was restless when we got home," I said.

"Got home from where?"

I told him about working with her and her new owner at the owner's house.

"What did she eat there?"

"Only the treats I brought with me."

"What do you *suspect* she ate?" Will said, his voice firm.

I turned and looked at him. His lips were compressed in a grim line, his eyes hard.

Doc ran a hand over his mostly bald head. "Was she extra thirsty?"

"Yes."

"Chocolate," Doc said. "And as bad as the reaction was, I'd say probably dark chocolate."

I whipped out my phone and punched numbers.

"It's kinda late," Will said.

"I don't care."

"Hello." Rainey's voice, sounding timid.

"This is Marcia. Did you give Lacy anything to eat today, besides the treats I gave you?"

"What? No. Why? What's wrong?"

"She's in the hospital, that's what's wrong. Somebody gave her chocolate."

"Nooo." A long wail. "I'd never do that. I know chocolate's bad for dogs." A beat of silence. "Is she okay?" Rainey's voice quavered.

And my anger drained away, at her at least. I believed her. Rainey might be unstable, but she wouldn't intentionally do anything to harm Lacy.

"The doc thinks so. But she's not going to be up for training tomorrow." And maybe not for a while after that, but I kept that thought to myself.

Snuffling in my ear.

I softened my voice. "She's young and she's strong, and Doc Murdock's the best veterinarian I know. I'll call you tomorrow with an update, okay?"

"Okay." Her voice was small, that of a scared child.

"She'll be fine," I said, hoping that was true.

"Talk to you tomorrow."

Disconnecting, I looked up. Doc Murdock had wandered off.

Will patted my arm. "He said to call in the morning to check on Lacy."

We started for home. Will pulled into a fast food drive-thru. But worry about Lacy, combined with the smell from the backseat and my own clothes, made it hard to swallow down the burger and fries.

"This guy's like a ghost," Will said, when we were on the road again. "Somehow sneaking chocolate to Lacy. And sticking a nail in my tire, probably while I was sitting in the car."

"Probably? When weren't you sitting in it?"

"Only when I got out to get the muffin and tea. And then I

dumped the bucket behind that same bush, just before you came out. I didn't want us to have to smell it all the way home."

I snorted at the irony, since we now had our windows down to make the smell coming from the backseat bearable.

"We don't know that the nail is connected," I reminded him. "It could be a coincidence."

He glanced my way. "Lawmen are inherently suspicious of coincidences."

"Yeah, but they do happen. And nobody could've just slipped chocolate to Lacy. She's been taught never to eat anything I don't approve."

I fell silent. I had given the dog the okay to take food from Rainey.

Will's thoughts must have been tracking along the same lines. "Are you sure your client didn't give her some?" he asked.

I nodded, although I wasn't as sure as I had been earlier. "Rainey called this guy an ebola virus today, spreading to everybody she touches."

"That analogy works too," Will said through gritted teeth.

When we got to the house, I waved a hand toward the backseat. "I'll help you clean up in a few minutes, but I need to tend to the dogs first, okay?"

He nodded and headed for his trunk. I hoped he had a shovel in there, because he was going to need it to get the mess out of his car.

I let Jenny out first while I freshened her water bowl. Then I settled her in her crate for the night.

Motioning to Buddy to follow me, I nabbed my half-empty wineglass on the way by. I flipped the switch for the floodlights that illuminated the backyard and pushed open the screen door.

Buddy bolted from bush to bush, sniffing but not stopping to pee. His frantic searching said he really needed to go, so I couldn't quite figure out why he was being so picky about finding just the right spot.

I strolled behind him, trying to unwind from one of the worst days of my life. I willed my muscles to relax, and most of them cooperated. I rolled my head around on my shoulders to get the stiffness out of my neck.

At the magnolia tree, guilt niggled at my stomach. I should be helping Will clean out his car. I chugged the last of my wine.

Buddy suddenly turned and bolted back toward the house, his nose down.

What the heck…

I pivoted, my gaze following his path all the way to the house. I expected him to stop and pee on the tiger lilies blooming there, but instead he plunged through them and jumped up on the side of the house, barking.

My eyes moved upward and the wineglass slipped from my hand. A scream erupted from my throat.

CHAPTER EIGHT

Buddy ran back to me, stopped, sniffed at the wineglass in the grass. Amazingly, it hadn't broken.

"Leave it!" My voice was far harsher than I'd intended.

Buddy lifted his head and tilted it to one side.

I flopped down on my butt and threw my arms around his neck.

Will bolted out the back door. "What happened?" he yelled.

I looked up, opened my mouth, but nothing came out.

He pounded across the lawn and came to a stop next to me. "You okay? Why'd you scream?"

I lifted a hand and pointed at the house.

This guy was no graffiti artist. Again, the letters were sloppy and ran off the edge of the wall.

LAST WARNING. STAY OUT OF OCAL…

Will cussed under his breath. Then strong fingers encircled my upper arm and lifted me gently to my feet. I kept one hand entwined in Buddy's fur and turned my face against Will's chest.

I loved my little house. It felt like someone had thrown paint on my child. Tears stung my eyes. My stomach roiled, threatening to give back my dinner and the wine.

Will had an arm firmly around my shoulders as he eyed the damage. "You still think the nail was a coincidence?" His voice simmered with barely suppressed anger.

"What?" My overwhelmed brain failed to see the connection.

"The nail was to slow us down so he could get here first and do this."

"Oh," I said as I continued to stare at my poor house.

Suddenly pain and fear morphed into anger. My vision blurred in a red haze and my chest felt like it might explode. "I'm going to get this guy," I growled, low and fierce.

Will turned me around, hands on both my shoulders. "No! *I'm* going to get this guy, and you're going to keep a low profile until I do."

I burst into tears.

He pulled me against his chest and wrapped his arms around me.

It was three a.m. by the time we went to bed.

Will had called the Marion County Sheriff's Department and had told them about the whole mess. Rainey's sister wouldn't be happy about that, but I didn't care at this point if she got arrested for drugs.

The fact that Will was also a local sheriff must have carried some clout, because not one but two cruisers pulled up out front thirty minutes later.

Some confusion ensued because of the previous call to Rainey's house, and my name being given as the owner there. Fingers crossed behind my back to negate the fib, I'd suggested that the deputy had been confused. "We were kinda both talking at once."

Not really. Rainey'd been doing most of the talking and I'd been doing most of the scowling.

Then two deputies and a crime scene tech had tromped all over my backyard and along my fence line. The tech even scraped some of Lacy's dried vomit off of Will's backseat to be analyzed.

Finally Will saw the deputies and technicians off. When he came back into the house, I was standing in the middle of my living room, trying to figure out how my life had turned to crap so fast.

"They found some scratches on the fence," Will said, "where

they think a ladder was hooked on it."

"Hooked?"

"Yeah, it might have been one of those kind you can get to drop out a bedroom window in case of fire."

"Which wouldn't be that easy to find down here, where so few houses have second floors."

"True." He put an arm around my shoulders and steered me toward my bedroom. "But one can order just about anything on the Internet."

I stopped our progress as we neared my bedroom door. "Uh, Will…"

He put a finger on my lips. "We're not doing anything tonight. I want our first time to be special."

I sighed gratefully and leaned against him, and almost gagged at the smell of his shirt.

He stepped back and stripped off the offending garment, then pulled me close and gave me a long, tender kiss. Certain parts of my body protested the postponement of more strenuous activities. But I knew if we tried to make love, I'd probably fall asleep in the middle of it.

"Would it be too torturous if we slept in the same bed?" I asked.

He pursed his lips, then gave me a small smile. "I think I can handle that. But I stay clothed." He looked down at his bare chest. "Well, mostly clothed and on the other side of the covers."

"Deal," I said, but my gaze was glued to his well-defined pecs, sprinkled with dark hairs.

Various body parts protested louder. I mentally told them to settle down.

I went in the bathroom and brushed my teeth, then changed into the oversized tee shirt I sleep in, wishing I had something more glamorous.

Will barely gave me a glance when I came out. "I hope you don't mind, but I threw my shirt in your washer."

I nodded as I covered a yawn.

Will carefully arranged the sheet and thin blanket on my bed so that I was under them and he wasn't. Then he rolled onto his side and kissed me gently on the lips. "Goodnight, Marcia."

"Night," I mumbled, my eyelids already drifting closed.

He laid a bare arm over my middle. I snuggled as close as the bedding between us allowed, wishing again that I had the energy to do something about my tingling body.

And that was my last thought until morning.

I woke to an empty bed and a medley of morning fragrances. Fresh air drifting in through the open window brought the subtle scent of spring flowers. And a delicious combination of aromas—of brewing coffee, hot grease and toasted bread—wafted from the kitchen. My stomach growled.

Buddy was lying on the rug beside my bed, head raised and nose quivering.

"Go on, boy." He bolted for the kitchen.

I took a lightning-fast shower and threw on my favorite red tank top and a clean pair of jeans.

The clatter of pans and clinking of china made me suspect that breakfast was being dished up. I rounded the corner into the kitchen and burst out laughing.

Will had dug a pink ruffled bib apron out of a kitchen drawer and had donned it over his jeans and now wrinkled but clean chambray shirt. The result was beyond ridiculous.

"Hey, it's your apron." He dropped two plates on the table and returned to the counter to get the coffee pot.

"My sister-in-law gave it to me for Christmas last year, and I wouldn't be caught dead in it."

Will grinned at me. "I let Buddy out, but I wasn't sure I should mess with Jenny."

"No, you shouldn't. Thank you." I went and got Jenny out of her crate and let her out back. "She can romp around a bit while we eat."

I plopped down in my chair and grabbed the fork from beside

the plate.

Will poured the coffee and joined me.

I was already gobbling eggs like there was no tomorrow. They were delicious and I said so.

"It's the hot sauce."

I stopped in mid-gobble. "Seriously? They don't taste spicy."

"No, 'cause you should always use a light touch. It just brings out the eggs' natural flavor that way."

I rolled my eyes toward the ceiling. "Thank you, Jesus, for this man!"

"Careful or Mrs. Wells will get after you for taking the Lord's name in vain."

"No way 'in vain.' I am truly grateful to the universe. You like red-headed women with big hips and you can cook."

"Your hips are not that big."

I frowned at him. "Not *that* big."

"As you said, I like them big. Gives me something to hang onto when I kiss you." He gave me a lascivious grin.

My nether regions perked up. "Um, you realize we now have the whole day to ourselves." I wiggled my eyebrows at him.

"Hm, I need to interview Mrs. Wells after breakfast. See if she noticed anything unusual yesterday."

"Ah, but she won't be home until church is out, about twelve-thirty." I glanced at the clock over my sink. "And it's only nine-fifteen."

"Um, there's something else I didn't get a chance to go home and pack yesterday."

"What's that?"

"Condoms."

"Oh."

A woof from the kitchen doorway. Jenny stood outside the screen.

I knew just how she felt–tongue hanging out, panting.

I called the animal hospital and was told that Lacy was doing better. Doc Murdock said she should make a full recovery, but he wanted to keep her until Monday for observation.

Will blew out a huge sigh of relief when I told him.

He helped out with Jenny's morning training session, playing the part of a passerby trying to engage her. He reached out his hand as if to pet her. I inserted my own hand between her and him. She touched her nose to my palm, then looked to me for further instruction.

I resisted the urge to sing *Hallelujah* as I gently led her away from Will. She was truly getting it that she should never let anyone distract her from her job.

We repeated several variations of the scenario, with Buddy watching from the shade of the magnolia tree. Jenny continued to stay focused on me, with only minor reminders with the nose-touch signal.

I gave her the release signal, then rewarded her with some treats and a big hug around the neck.

She trotted over to Will. He squatted down and gave her a thorough scratch behind her ears.

"How do you stand to let them go?" he asked.

"It's not easy." That reminded me of Lacy. My throat tightened at the thought of how close I had come to losing her in a very different way.

And that, in turn, reminded me that I hadn't called Rainey yet.

I pulled out my phone and made the call. I got voicemail, which was fine by me. I wasn't really in the mood to talk to her anyway. I left a message that Lacy was better but would need several days to recuperate. "I'll keep you posted."

"Speaking of Lacy recuperating," Will said as I disconnected, "you'll be tied down for a while with a sick dog once she comes home. How about I take you out to dinner later, while you can still go out? My new deputy's on duty tonight, but hopefully all will stay calm in Collins County."

Normally I would be delighted by such an invitation. Dog training at your own home is a lonely job. But I honestly didn't have the energy to go out. Despite the boon of spending time with Will, the previous day's events had me a little depressed.

"Truth be told, I'd rather eat in tonight."

"Then how about carryout? Chinese okay?"

He caught my hand and pulled me to him for a kiss. It felt good to melt against him and forget my problems.

He broke the kiss and grinned down at me. "I'll stop at a drugstore too, and pick up that little necessity I didn't have a chance to pack."

Now *that* brought a smile to my face.

Woohoo, I'm finally gonna get laid! my inner harlot chortled.

I told her to calm down. The way things had been going lately, I wasn't counting on anything until it happened.

He glanced at his watch. "But before I go, I need to talk to Mrs. Wells. Find out if she saw anything yesterday."

I took Jenny inside and put her in her crate with fresh water. She gratefully flopped down on her bed for a nap.

Then Will and I went out front and knocked on Mrs. Wells's door. Sherie Wells was the quintessential nosy neighbor, but I'd discovered recently that nosy neighbors had their good points.

She answered, still in her church clothes–a straight skirt of royal blue and matching snug jacket that flattered her curves and added to her natural regal air. A navy pillbox hat perched jauntily on her head in front of her chignon. The tailored suit was timeless. The hat was definitely a relic from the fifties.

Her mahogany skin was relatively wrinkle-free, despite the fact that she had grown children. I could only hope I aged half so well.

"Oh, Marcia, I saw all the hubbub last night and wondered what was goin' on. But I didn't want to get in the way." Her Southern accent was slight, despite having grown up in Mayfair. I knew she'd gone north for college and suspected she'd actively cultivated more accent-less speech patterns while there, and since then while teaching fifth graders their three Rs.

"Actually, ma'am," Will said. "We wanted to ask you some

questions about all that."

Warmth spread through my chest at his use of *we*.

"Why, Sheriff Haines, where are my manners? Y'all come on in." Now her Southern was showing a bit more.

We stepped into a living room jammed full of overstuffed furniture that matched the vintage of her hat. She gestured toward the sofa and we sat down.

"Can I get y'all some sweet tea?"

"No thanks, ma'am," I said.

Will cleared his throat. "Ms. Wells, did you see anyone hanging around Marcia's house yesterday afternoon?"

"I didn't see a person, but I saw that car again. Couldn't tell who was drivin' though."

"The green sedan?" I asked, then turned to Will. "She saw it out front the other day. We both thought it was somebody interested in the house next door."

Mrs. Wells was nodding.

"Did you see the license plate?" Will asked.

"They drove away fast when they saw me lookin' out the door. I only saw the first letter, a P."

He pulled a small pad and short pencil out of his shirt pocket. "When you say sedan, how big? A compact, mid-sized...?"

Mrs. Well's gave a slight shake of her head. "I don't know much about cars. It was kind of average size, I guess. Not real big but not real small either. And it wasn't new. The paint was dull."

Will was jotting notes onto the pad. "That's real helpful, ma'am."

"So what happened? What'd they do?"

Will shot me a warning glance that was hardly necessary. I wasn't going to feed the Mayfair rumor mill any more than I had to. But I needed Mrs. Wells to be on the alert, in case this guy came back.

"I need you to keep this confidential," I said, knowing full well that wasn't likely to happen.

She nodded her head, a little too vigorously, although her

expression remained neutral. She would consider it rude to appear too avidly interested, even though she was exactly that.

The pillbox hat hadn't moved one iota. It didn't dare.

I chose my words carefully. "The client I trained Lacy for, she's being stalked. And for some reason, this guy has latched onto me as some kind of threat. He's white, medium build with blond hair and blue eyes. Do you remember how tall he is, Will?"

"Six foot."

She shook her head. "That's a description that would fit a lot of people."

"True, but he won't be from around here. I'm pretty sure he lives in Ocala. And he's probably in his thirties."

I was realizing how little I'd actually gotten out of Rainey Bryant about this guy. Had she intentionally deflected me, or did we both just get caught up in her bad memories?

"So what happened last night?" Mrs. Wells asked again.

"Oh, sorry." I figured I might as well tell her. If she stood on her deck and raised up on her toes, she could see the red letters over the fence. "This guy spray-painted a warning on the back of my house."

Her eyes went wide and her mouth fell open.

Will took a business card from his jeans pocket and handed it to Mrs. Wells. "If you see anyone hanging around who doesn't belong, let me or Marcia know. My cell number's on the back. Don't worry about the time of day or night. You see something that looks funny, you call."

"I most certainly will, Sheriff."

Will and I stood up, announcing our departure.

Mrs. Wells stayed seated for a beat. I knew she would have loved to pump me for more juicy details, but good manners won out. She stood and showed us to the door.

"Thanks for your help, ma'am." Will sketched her a small salute.

"My pleasure, Sheriff, and I'll keep my eyes peeled."

Will took my hand as we stepped down off her porch. I tried

to pull away but he hung on.

"You know she's watching," I hissed quietly.

"Yup. I want her to know that I'm courting you."

"Courting me? How quaint." I snickered. "Hey, do you ever think about the phrases we use, how odd they are? Keeping one's eyes peeled. It brings up images of somebody whipping out a potato peeler and then plopping eyeballs into a pan of boiling water."

Will looked down at me, his mouth twisted in a wry smile. "You have a strange mind."

My stomach clenched. My own smile shifted from genuine to fake. I tried to keep my tone light. "I've been told that before."

He flashed me a full-blown grin, complete with sexy dimples. "I like that about you."

I laughed out loud, my insides relaxing.

"I know it's too early for dinner yet, but I think I'll go run those errands now." He wiggled his eyebrows at me. "We can put the Chinese in the fridge and heat it up later."

My stomach did a little flip, for a completely different reason this time. Warmth spread through my body, leaving a tingling sensation in its wake. "Uh, that sounds good. Then we can just *relax* all afternoon."

His grin was back. We'd reached my front door. He leaned down and gave me a chaste peck on the cheek. "That's exactly what I had in mind."

A half hour later my phone rang. Caller ID told me it was Will. I wandered out the back door as I answered, expecting him to ask what I wanted from the Chinese place.

"I'm afraid I've got some bad news," he said.

My body tensed. *What now?*

"My new deputy called me. He's resigning without notice."

My heart plummeted to my shoes. "Why?"

I plopped down on the wobbly wrought iron chair that matched my equally wobbly bistro table, both victims of a recent close encounter with an alligator.

Buddy had followed me out and settled at my feet.

"Another department where he'd applied called him and offered half again what I can pay him, plus more opportunities for advancement, but he had to start right away."

"It's been over a week since he started with you. Doesn't he realize he's their second choice?"

"Probably, but apparently we were his second choice." The desolation in his voice made my throat hurt.

"Well, it's not the end of the world." I tried for an upbeat tone, but probably fell a few feet short of that mark. "You'll find somebody else."

"Yeah, but I'm back to square one. And here's the really bad news."

My body sagged. I'd already guessed what was coming. "What?"

"Now I have to cover the three to eleven shift tonight."

"Can't you get somebody else to do it?"

"Not without paying overtime I can't afford. Everybody else has already worked their forty hours this week. And they have families. I don't want to suddenly pull them away from their kids on a Sunday."

I made a face at the phone, wishing he wasn't such a conscientious boss.

"The good news is, I got the condoms. I'm gonna keep them in the glove compartment of my car."

"Okay, good… Did you get all the mess out of your car?"

"Yeah, I took it to the car wash and hauled the backseat out and hosed it down."

"Hope it doesn't get moldy on you."

"I'll leave the windows open tonight. It's not supposed to rain."

We both knew the mundane conversation was only putting off the inevitable.

"Well, I guess I'd better head down there. I'll text you later."

"Okay. Take care." I disconnected.

Buddy must have sensed my mood because he sat up on his haunches and put his head in my lap. I stroked his soft ears, contemplating my life. Then I flopped back in the chair.

It almost went over backward. I really needed to replace the deck furniture.

Yeah, ain't gonna happen any time soon.

Without the payment for training Lacy, the budget was going to be ultra tight for a while.

I glanced up at the red letters on my house. My chest filled with an echo of the rage I'd felt last night.

This s.o.b., whoever he was, had screwed up my life royally.

Sorry, Mom, I apologized in my head for coming even that close to cussing.

My parents had been loving but strict–my mom liked to call it *firm*. I'd been taught not to curse, lie or steal. And most of all, I'd been taught not to intentionally cause another person bodily harm.

But right now, I wanted to track this guy down and throttle him with my bare hands.

I needed to know more about him. My hands fisted on top of the table.

Since I now had a free afternoon stretching in front of me, I was going to find out that information. I needed to talk to Rainey, and not over the phone. I wanted to see her face when I asked her my questions, so I'd know if she was lying.

I wasn't sure why I distrusted her. I guess the whole pretending her house was mine to the deputy had a lot to do with it.

I jumped up and went back in the house. Grabbing Buddy's leash from its hook, I gestured to him and headed out the front. Despite the writing on the wall, we were going to Ocala.

CHAPTER NINE

I hoped having Buddy along would discourage Rainey's stalker from trying anything. There was enough Rottweiler mixed in with his Black Labrador genes to give him some of the tell-tale tan markings of a Rottie. Most people weren't about to mess with him.

Of course the stalker might retaliate later, but I was pissed enough at this point, I was willing to take that chance. I wasn't going to sit around my house watching my bank balance shrink to nothing while he played head games with Rainey.

I parked at the opposite end of the block from where Will had parked yesterday and called Rainey.

When she answered, I said without preamble, "I need to talk to you."

"Carrie's here. Can I call you back?"

"No. I'm in my car down the block. This will only take a few minutes. Turn right when you come out of your house."

"Are we going somewhere?" Her voice shook a little.

I softened my tone. "No. I just have a couple of questions to ask you."

"Can Carrie come?"

"No. I need to talk to you alone."

A few seconds of silence. "Okay."

A minute later, she came out on her porch and walked down the sidewalk. I think she was trying to look like she was just out for a stroll, but I could see the tension in her body from half a block away. Her head swiveled back and forth on her neck, like a puppeteer's marionette.

I felt a little guilty for forcing an agoraphobic woman out of her house, but only a little.

When she was parallel with my car I clicked the passenger door open.

She got in without looking at me. "How's Lacy doing?"

"Better. Did you get my message?"

She nodded, staring straight ahead, her body stiff. I wasn't sure if she was pissed at me or on the verge of an anxiety attack.

"Rainey," I said in as gentle a voice as I could muster. "I need you to tell me this guy's name and as much about him as you can. Do you know where he lives?"

"Joe Fleming, Joseph. And I went to his old address today. His landlady said he'd moved."

"What?" How the heck had this woman, who was about to fly apart sitting outside her own house, gotten up the nerve to drive somewhere? Then again, maybe her earlier excursion was why she was now a basketcase.

"Carrie went with me."

Okay, that made more sense.

Rainey turned on the passenger seat so she was half facing me, and jumped a little in her seat. Her head jerked toward the back. Apparently she hadn't noticed the big dog lying on the backseat when she got in.

And she was definitely not in good shape.

"That's Buddy," I said. "He's a real sweetie. Would you like to pet him?"

She froze a beat, then nodded.

I patted the console between the front seats. Buddy stretched out his paws onto it and laid his head on his legs.

Rainey put a hand tentatively on his head. His tail thumped against the backseat. She stroked his soft black ear.

"Is he a Rottweiler?"

"About one quarter. He's mostly Black Lab."

She stroked his ears some more and visibly settled down.

I asked her for this Fleming's old address and wrote it down. "Did his landlady know where he'd moved to?"

"No... Marcia, I've been thinking and I'm having trouble believing he'd do all this. Harass me with phone calls or notes, maybe, which is how it all started. But he never seemed violent to me. And why would he go after you and poor Lacy?"

"He wants you off kilter. He doesn't want you to get a service dog, since that will help you be less nervous."

"But see, that's what doesn't fit. Joe loves dogs. That's one of the things we had in common. And he was really excited that I was getting a service dog. That is, before we broke up."

"How old is this guy?" I asked.

"He's a couple of years older than me. Thirty-three."

"What kind of car does he drive?" I asked.

"A blue Honda. He got it last year."

Dang, I was hoping for a green sedan, but that would've been too easy. "He bought it new?"

"Yeah, I think so. It looked pretty new." She continued to stroke Buddy's ears.

He moaned softly.

Rainey's and my eyes met, and we both smiled.

"I think he likes that," I said.

Her smile widened into a full-blown grin. "Ya think?"

I looked down at Buddy and gave him an indulgent shake of my head. Then my mood sobered. "Okay, I'm going to try to track this Joe Fleming down and see what I can find out."

"You said he spray-painted your house too. I'm so sorry, Marcia." Rainey's eyes had gone wide, her mouth now a grim line. She seemed genuinely stricken.

I patted her hand, still resting on Buddy's head. "It's not your fault."

"No. But you were dragged into this because of me, and now who knows when I'll get Lacy."

"On that subject, did you feed her anything but the treats I gave you?" I'd asked her that before, over the phone, but I wanted to see her face when she answered.

"No." Her gaze was steady, her expression sober. No twitches or eyes darting away.

"Did you leave her unattended at any point?" We'd been assuming that Lacy had eaten whatever made her sick, but maybe someone injected her with something.

"I went to the bathroom while you were outside, but I took her with me. I didn't want her to freak out in a relatively strange house without either one of us around."

I gave her an encouraging smile. "That was good thinking. Did you have the treats with you the whole time?"

"Yeah. I put them in a bowl to take back outside. But they got kinda soggy, sitting in the sun."

Hmm, that made me wonder if the treats had simply gone bad. They were a little on the soft side normally, but not what one would call soggy.

"You set the bowl on the picnic table?"

Rainey nodded.

The guy would indeed have to be a ghost then, to sneak over to them behind Rainey's back, and without a reaction from Lacy. And what could he have doctored them with that wouldn't be obvious? Rainey would have noticed if they were suddenly covered in chocolate syrup.

Maybe the treats had indeed gone bad, and Lacy's illness was a coincidence, not caused by the stalker.

"Okay, thanks for all your help." I patted her hand again. "I'm going to do my best to find this guy and put him out of business. Then you and I can both get on with our lives."

I glanced out the windshield and tensed. Carrie was walking along the sidewalk from Rainey's porch to the street. Today, she wore denim shorts and a light blue tank top, so tight they looked painted on. Her long legs were a smooth, even tan.

My lip curled.

Why do I dislike her so? All she'd done was try to pet a cute dog.

The sun glinted off her bright red curls. My hair had red high-lights, but it couldn't compare to this woman's lustrous locks.

Heat crept up my face. I was jealous of her appearance, plain and simple.

Carrie had stopped at the mailbox and was looking around.

"There's your friend." I tilted my head forward.

Rainey followed my line of vision and smiled.

"Thanks for being so understanding, Marcia." She leaned over and gave me a quick hug. "I know you didn't bargain on a stalker when you signed on to train me."

This time, the hug didn't feel so awkward.

She got out of the car and walked toward her house.

She needs her dog. She'd calmed down substantially just pet-ting Buddy.

I was even more determined to bring an end to this stalker's reign of terror.

As I was mulling over the best way to get this Joe Fleming's new address, Rainey reached her mailbox.

Carrie gave her that big toothy smile. She threw an arm around Rainey's shoulders, and they moved together up the walk, heads bent, chatting.

My cheeks heated again. I'd thought I was a better person than that. My little spurts of Becky envy weren't that hard to quell. But then I knew Becky well, knew she was a good and kind person.

I vowed to give Carrie Williams the benefit of the doubt.

I yanked my mind back to the dilemma of how to find Joe Fleming. Will could easily get his new address, but I didn't want to wait to confront this guy. And once Will was in the loop, he'd want me to back away from it.

I appreciated his desire to protect me, but this guy had made it personal when he'd messed up my house. And if it turned out he was responsible for Lacy getting sick, *he* might be the one Will needed to protect from physical harm, at my hands.

I plugged Joseph Fleming and Ocala into the search engine on my phone. I got twenty-eight hits. A few could be ruled out based on age, but it would still take me days to check out the rest of them.

I entered his old address into my GPS. I drove there and then plugged in the addresses for each of the most likely Joseph Flemings from my Internet search, the ones that were under forty and single. Four of them were less than five miles away. The rest were a good bit further.

If only I could find out which of these guys owned a late model blue Honda. I wished I was like those private investigators on TV, who always had a friend in the Department of Motor Vehicles.

I messed around online some more with my phone and found a website that ran background checks, for a fee of course. But they had a one-time free trial. Hmm, maybe I'd save that for after I'd narrowed these Joe Flemings down to one or two.

I drove to the first address, then unhooked Buddy from his safety strap and slipped his service vest on. Since I planned to pose as a post office employee, it would seem strange that I'd brought my pet along, but a service dog was a different story. Of course the fact that it was Sunday was likely to cause some skepticism.

The man who answered the door looked a bit rough. He was a big guy, and yes, he was a blue-eyed blond, but the stubble on his jowly cheeks was mostly gray. The online info had said he was in his late thirties but I'd put him closer to mid to late forties.

I launched into my spiel. "Sir, I'm doing a survey for the U.S. Postal Service regarding their mail-forwarding system. Did you used to live at 2515 Mayburn Avenue here in Ocala?"

"What is this? Some kinda scam? And what's with the dog?"

He gave me no chance to answer any of his questions. The door slammed shut. But that was fine. He hadn't resembled the smiling young man in Rainey's photo.

I wished I still had the photo, but it was now in Will's possession.

The second guy was more polite, barely. He also didn't look

much like the photo image, but he was in his thirties. After silently listening to my spiel, he shook his head and closed his door.

I scored on the third try. The guy looked like the photo dude's older brother–it's amazing how much a frown ages one. "Yeah, I lived there until four months ago. Why?"

"Have you been getting your mail forwarded okay?"

He crossed his arms in front of his chest.

I discreetly slipped my left foot over the threshold, in case he decided to close the door on me.

"I never submitted a forwarding order."

"Oh."

Now what? Okay, time for honesty.

"Are you the Joe Fleming who used to date Rainey Bryant?"

"What?" He dropped his arms and leaned forward a little. I think his intention was to force me to back up, but I resisted the urge.

"Who *are* you?" he said through gritted teeth. His blue eyes were icy.

"Look, I just want to ask you a couple of questions about a situation that's come up with Rainey."

He stood frozen in his angry pose for a few seconds. Then he sighed and stepped back. "Come in."

"I'd, um, rather you came out. I noticed a little park down the block. Could we walk down there and talk?"

He looked at his feet. They were bare. "Lemme get my shoes."

I stepped back and he pushed the door shut. I was half expecting him to throw the lock and let me rot on his doorstep. But about thirty seconds later, he opened the door and came out, now wearing flip-flops.

We headed down the sidewalk, Buddy at my left knee, Mr. Fleming to my right.

He gestured toward Buddy. "Are you with the people who are getting Rainey her dog?"

"Yes, but we can't turn the dog over to her yet, because she's been having problems."

He let out a short bark of humorless laughter. "I thought that's why she needed the dog, because she has problems."

"Well, she's had some random things happen to her lately. Some anonymous calls and then last week somebody spray-painted a threat on her house."

He stopped walking and turned toward me, worry flickering in his eyes. "I'm sorry to hear that."

"We can't give her the dog until we're sure it will be safe with her." I nodded down toward Buddy. "A lot of expensive training goes into these animals, and we care about what happens to them."

I was working hard to keep my tone pleasant. Anger was building in my chest. If this guy had poisoned Lacy, I might just rip his face off.

He started moving again. "She doesn't have any idea who's doing this stuff?"

"Well, yes. She thought it might be you."

He shook his head but kept walking. "Somehow I thought that was coming. Rainey gives drama queen a whole new definition."

I silently agreed with him.

When he kept walking in silence, I said, "She told me you broke up with her, over sex issues, but then called her to get back together."

"About half true. I broke up with her, but not over sex. I understood that she needed to call the shots there, considering what happened to her." He glanced toward me. "You know what happened, right?"

I nodded.

"And I didn't call her. She called me. Despite the drama and her jealousy, I was leaning toward getting back together."

"She's the jealous type?" I didn't find that hard to believe.

"Yeah, she'd get worked up whenever I even glanced in the direction of another woman. But it was all coming from her insecurities. I understood that. I might have taken her back, if the weird calls hadn't started."

"Weird calls?"

"Yeah, three of them. The voice was disguised, you know, with one of those gizmos, so it sounded all tinny. But I think it was a guy. Told me to stay away from Rainey."

"Did he threaten to do anything to you if you didn't?"

"No, just a generic 'or else.' I figured she'd hooked up with somebody new, who was as jealous as she was. I wasn't in the mood to end up in some crazy triangle, so I left her alone." Joe's gaze flicked in my direction. "How's she doing?"

"Not all that great right now, although I'm learning that she has a lot of inner strength."

We had reached the park. He gestured toward a bench and I sat. Buddy plopped his butt down next to my feet.

Fleming left a polite foot of bench between us. "Yeah, I think she does," he said.

"Does what?"

"Have inner strength. She had to in order to survive all she's been through."

"You mean the Army and all?"

"Well, that but as a kid too. Both her parents running off like they did."

First I'd heard of that version. "She told me her parents were dead."

"That's her cover story, but her father left when she was real little. She doesn't even remember him. Then when she was eight, her mother dumped her on a neighbor and left the state."

"No wonder she's a mess," I mumbled. I hadn't meant to say it out loud.

"Yeah." He sat quietly for a few moments, leaning forward, his knees spread, his gaze on the ground between his feet. "Why'd she think it was me?"

"Her sister thought she saw you running away from the house, right before they discovered the graffiti."

"Ah, Sunny." He threw his arms up in the air.

"What?" I said when he didn't elaborate.

"She's so overprotective. She drove me nuts."

"What do you mean?"

"Like one time, Rainey had a mild cold, and Sunny convinced her not to go out with me. Then she turns to me, all sweetness and light." His face twisted in a parody of a polite smile. "'You'd better go, Joe,'" he screeched in a bad imitation of a female voice, "'before you catch her germs.'

"And one time last summer, we were supposed to meet for a movie after I got off from work." Joe was on a roll, his eyes flashing with anger. "Sunny took her car to run errands, so Rainey had no wheels."

Sounded like a simple miscommunication to me.

"I had to go get her, by which time the movie had already started–"

"Hey wait, what about her agoraphobia?" I blurted out.

"Her what?"

I felt heat creeping up my cheeks, but the damage was already done. "Her fear of going out by herself."

"That's a new one."

"Huh?"

"She was anxious about a lot of stuff, but that wasn't one of them, at least not during the day or when she was meeting someone."

Interesting. Was her agoraphobia a new development since the stalking? That would make sense, and also explain why she could still make herself go out at times, if the disorder wasn't full blown.

Yet. Agoraphobia had a tendency to extend to more and more situations over time.

"Sunny doesn't have a car?" I asked.

"She doesn't need one most of the time, since she works at home." Joe seemed to have calmed down. He was back to sounding like Mr. Nice Guy.

"What does she do for a living?" I asked.

"Rainey said she sells things, on eBay. Stuff she buys at yard sales and such."

I was tempted to ask if he'd ever seen signs of drugs around the house. But Rainey, as flaky as she could be, had never seemed to be stoned or high on anything. And whatever Sunny might be doing drug-wise really wasn't my business. I reined in my idle curiosity.

About that, at least. "What about Rainey's friend, Carrie Williams? She was there the day the graffiti was discovered."

Joe was quiet for a beat. "Carrie's okay."

"But…"

"No, no buts."

"Then what?"

His face turned red. Embarrassment? Or anger about my questions?

"She and I went out a couple of times, that's all. Since Rainey and I broke up."

"A couple of times?"

"Maybe three. It's nothing serious."

"Does Carrie know where you live?"

Joe shifted to look at me. His face had returned to its normal color. "No. We've always met somewhere, but she has my cell number."

Hmm, I wondered if Carrie's willingness to accompany Rainey to Joe's old abode was purely altruistic.

He ducked his head. "Last time she called, I told her I couldn't meet her, that I was really busy with work."

I let the silence hang between us. I'd heard somewhere, or maybe read it in a book, that staying quiet was a great way to get someone you're interrogating to let something slip.

"What did the graffiti say?" Joe asked.

"I'm gonna get you, B-I-T."

"Bit?"

"Yeah, he ran out of room on the wall. This guy's no graphic designer."

Fleming chuckled softly and shook his head. "My dad was a cop. He used to say that most criminals get caught because they're downright stupid."

Color me confused. Was this guy our stalker? He'd shown no signs of recognizing me. And except for his outburst about Sunny, he'd seemed pretty sane, not the violent type.

If he was lying, he was a darn good actor.

Then again, in my abnormal psych class in grad school, we'd talked about pathological liars. They could often fool you, because the line between truth and fiction had become so blurred for them that they believed their own lies.

And if Joe Fleming wasn't the stalker, then who was?

"Can you think of anybody who might stalk Rainey, a former boyfriend maybe?"

Joe was quiet for a moment, his eyes unfocused. Then he shook his head. "It would have to be from a long time ago. I think I'm the only one she's dated since the Army."

"In the Army?"

He shook his head again.

"Do you happen to know the name of the guy who assaulted her?"

He stiffened. "Yeah. She used to have nightmares. She'd yell out his name." He imitated someone flailing around. "'Get off me, Sergeant. Stop, Connors.'" He turned to me. His lips were pressed together in a thin line. "His name is Scott Connors."

I walked away from that interview very unsure of one thing, and pretty sure about another.

CHAPTER TEN

I was pretty sure Joe Fleming still had feelings for Rainey Bryant. And he was definitely capable of harassing phone calls and notes, but was he likely to do anything more aggressive than that?

Maybe to Sunny, whom he obviously didn't like, but to Rainey?

Once in my car, I used my free trial on the background check site to order a report on Joe.

Will would no doubt do a background check on him, but he might or might not share the results with me.

I pointed my car toward home. It being Sunday, traffic was a bit lighter on southbound I-75. I settled into the middle lane, then called Will at his office.

"Sheriff Haines."

"Hey, how's it going?"

"Pretty boring actually. Law enforcement in Collinsville often is."

"Well, I've got a couple of names for you. One's the guy who assaulted Rainey. His name's Scott Connors."

"One step ahead of you there. I already got my hands on the report from the Army investigation. They didn't want to give it to me, but one of our commissioners knows a general."

"So the flakes come in handy at times?"

"Yeah, sometimes," Will said. "Connors is stationed at Camp Blanding now, as a National Guard trainer."

"Crapola! That's near Starke, isn't it?"

"Yup. And he lives off base, just south of Starke, barely an hour's drive from Ocala."

"I hope Rainey doesn't know he's that close by," I said. "That would really freak her out."

"I got something else on him, something the general told Commissioner Evans. Connors was not officially punished for the assault, but enough of the brass believed he'd done it to put an unofficial black mark next to his name. He hasn't been promoted since then."

I maneuvered around a tractor-trailer and moved back into the middle lane. "I thought sergeant was as high as you could go as a non-com anyway."

"Apparently there are eight different levels," Will said. "Connors is stuck at staff sergeant, the second one up."

"Hmm, gives him good motivation for revenge, doesn't it? What's his address?"

A beat of silence. "Why? *You're* not going to get anywhere near him."

Oops!

"No, of course not," I quickly said.

"What's the other name, her former boyfriend?"

"Yeah. It's Joseph Fleming, but I'm not sure he's the stalker type."

"And why is that?" His voice had a hard edge to it. I could visualize him narrowing his eyes.

"Well, Rainey doesn't think it's him. She says he's not that way."

"Say hundreds of battered women a day, in Florida alone."

"True, but..."

"What have you done, Marcia?"

"Uh..." There's a downside, I realized, to Will understanding me so well.

A horn blared. I flinched and jerked my head in that direction. The semi I'd just passed was now bearing down on me in the right lane, and my car had wandered dangerously close to the line.

Heart pounding, I wrenched the steering wheel to the left, back into the center of my own lane. The semi blasted by me.

"Hey, I'm driving. Let me call you back when I get home." I disconnected before he had a chance to respond.

From a road safety standpoint, it was the best thing to do. From an avoiding Will's wrath standpoint, it was probably a bad move.

I put off calling Will back, telling myself that Jenny needed my attention. Some clouds rolled in as a last-gasp cold front from up north collided with the tropical air from the south. Thunderstorms were predicted, so I decided to work inside.

I took Jenny into my bedroom. I told her to lie down next to the bed and pretended I was going to take a nap.

Once she was asleep, I started moaning and thrashing in the bed, as if I were having a nightmare.

She barked once, and the next thing I knew she was standing on my chest, licking my face.

"No, girl." I gently shoved her off the bed.

She had the basic idea. She was supposed to wake me up, but jumping up on a combat veteran having a nightmare was likely to get her tossed across the room.

"Buddy. Come here, boy."

The scratching of his claws as he padded across the living room's terrazzo floor. Then he came around the corner into the bedroom.

I pointed across the room. "Jenny, lie down over there."

She cocked her head at me, but Buddy nosed his way in between her and the bed. She moved over a few feet. He laid down next to the bed, and after a moment, she sank down where she was.

I stretched out on the bed and lay still for a few minutes. Then I moaned and thrashed.

Buddy woofed and put his front paws up on the side of the bed. He barked again and tapped my arm with a paw. I pretended to wake up, shook my head as if I were clearing it of a nightmare, and then patted him. "Good boy."

He and I demonstrated the desired behavior again. Then by pointing and several "go over there's" and "lie down here's," I got the dogs to change places, with some confused tilting of their heads.

This time when I faked a nightmare, Jenny had the idea. She barked and put her front paws up on the bed, nudging my arm with one of them. I thrashed a little more to see what she would do, but she just barked again.

I "woke up" and praised her, then gave her a treat.

I faked a few more nightmares. Twice Jenny tried to jump on the bed, but I blocked her. Finally she did it right six times in a row.

She was really coming along nicely and I told her so.

I'd left my phone on the kitchen counter, hooked to its charger. When I'd finished with Jenny, I checked it. There was a text from Will.

Something came up. Gonna be busy. Talk later.

My heart turned to lead and sank into my stomach.

I called Becky and after asking about her health–which she informed me was totally back to normal–I complained in her ear about Will.

She made appropriate BFF-type noises. But when I'd finally wound down, she asked, "Why *are* you checking into this yourself?"

I realized I hadn't yet told her about the previous day's events. They were topics a bit too complicated to explain in a text. I filled her in on Lacy first.

"Oh no! Is she going to be okay?"

"The vet thinks so. I'm to pick her up tomorrow afternoon. Beck, I also think you're getting sick wasn't food poisoning."

"What?"

"I got a very strange package in the mail Friday." I told her about the box of stained paper towels and the words painted on my poor house. "Whoever's stalking my client seems to have shifted his focus to me, or rather expanded his focus. He wants me to stay away from my client, which I can't do. I have to finish her training once Lacy is well enough to continue."

"You think this guy put something in my food, maybe got mixed up about who was sitting where?"

I unplugged my phone from its charger cord so I could pace around the kitchen. Buddy lay on the rug by the back door, his gaze following me as I walked back and forth. "No, I think the tea-stained paper towels weren't just to let me know the poisoning was intentional. There was something in the iced tea, and he probably put it in both glasses to make sure I got it."

"But the waitress had given you sweet tea, and you didn't drink it."

"Exactly."

Becky was silent for a moment. "So what do these suspects of yours look like? Should I be on guard?"

"I don't think he was intentionally coming after you, but yeah, you might want to be suspicious of blue-eyed blonds for the time being."

"Great." Becky let out a sound that was half snort, half laugh. "That eliminates about one quarter of the male population from my dating pool."

"Oh, and he's average height and build. So you can add the tall, skinny blonds and the short, fat ones back in."

She chuckled. "And the tall, fat ones and short, skinny ones."

Despite the grimness of the subjects we'd discussed, I was smiling when we said our goodbyes. Becky usually had that effect on me.

Monday morning was my bimonthly counseling session with Jo Ann Hamilton. She was down in Lakeland, a very long trek for me, but she was worth it. The whole counseling thing had started out to be about grief over the death of a client, but lately we'd meandered into "why don't I trust men" territory.

To me that was a no-brainer. My violinist ex-husband had cheated on me and when I'd confronted him, he'd ended up choosing that slut of a cello player over me. It had put me off symphony concerts and dating for the better part of three years.

But now there was Will, a powerful motivator to overcome my anxieties.

Of course, Jo Ann dove into that pool first. She'd no sooner ushered me into her rather Spartan office than she asked, "You two get it together yet?"

That's what I liked most about this woman. She didn't mince words. She did a lot of contract work for the Veterans Administration and working with veterans taught you early on not to mess around. Vets like straight shooters. And so do I.

I told her about the debacle of a weekend we'd had. "I am really trying to make it happen now, honest. I don't even feel uptight about it." Well, not very much. Probably about as much as anybody worries when they're going to do the big deed with a new lover for the first time.

Of course, explaining why we hadn't had a successful weekend brought up the issue of my client, Rainey. Without mentioning names, I summarized the eventful week that had led up to the crazy weekend.

"This woman sounds like she has borderline personality disorder," Jo Ann said.

That made me sit up in my chair. "Really?"

"The intensity, the volatile moods, the clinginess."

I tensed, suddenly feeling defensive for Rainey's sake. "But she's a nice person."

Jo Ann nodded. "Don't get me wrong, I like borderlines. Most therapists hate working with them, but I can look at them, and it's like this small, hurt child is looking back at me."

I sat further forward. "Yeah, exactly. She's like a little kid struggling to deal with these overwhelming adult situations."

Jo Ann picked up her mug from the little table next to her chair and took a sip of coffee. "Borderlines usually have a lot of abuse in their histories, and abandonment stuff. Either actual physical abandonment or the parents emotionally weren't there in a big way."

"Her parents both left her, when she was a kid. She lives with her… another relative." I'd almost said *sister*, and in the small world of folks who provide services for ex-military personnel, Jo Ann might have heard of Rainey and her particular circumstances.

Of course, anything I said in a session was confidential, but…

I was usually more careful about my clients' privacy, and it was starting to bother me that I kept blathering to anyone who would listen about Rainey.

Not anyone, I told myself, *only Will and Jo Ann.*

Oh, and some to Becky. And I'd probably said more than I should have to Joe Fleming.

I suppressed the urge to smack myself. When I'm stressed out, the first thing that goes is the little bit of impulse control I possess.

"Thanks for the diagnosis," I said. "I'd been leaning toward histrionic personality disorder." Sometimes, I just couldn't resist reminding Jo Ann that I had a psychology background too.

She waggled her hand back and forth in a same-same gesture. "There's not a huge difference between them. They're both usually melodramatic. But histrionics tend to be superficial in their relationships, while borderlines are clingy and demanding."

That definitely described Rainey.

"That helps a lot to understand where my client's coming from."

"Don't take it as gospel, though. It's kind of like armchair quarterbacking, to diagnose from afar."

"Still, it helps." I would try harder to be patient with Rainey.

"Now, then," Jo Ann propped an elbow on the arm of her chair and cupped her chin in her hand, "when *are* you going to do the hokey-pokey with this guy?"

Considering that we were barely speaking at the moment, the truthful answer was when Hades gets quite chilly. I'd called Will back first thing this morning. It went right to voicemail. We usually met for lunch on the Mondays when I have counseling, but there'd been no mention of that in our abortive communications lately.

I gave a nervous little laugh. "You're not going to let me off the hook, are you?"

Jo Ann shook her head without dislodging her chin from its perch. "Nope."

I had a choice to make. I could have a staring contest with her for the next half hour, a competition I was quite sure I would lose. Or I could go ahead and tell her what had happened most recently.

So I did. "Why is it that men feel like they are the only ones who can take risks when something's important to them?" I concluded.

Jo Ann sat back. "Good question. Probably because they assume they can handle themselves, and they perceive us as physically vulnerable."

"When in reality, we're not as helpless as they believe and they're not as invincible."

She nodded. "Well put. Of course, when you finally tell him what you did, he's gonna say you're messing in police business."

I snorted softly. "If this were a murder investigation, he'd have a point."

For a moment, my stomach churned with old guilt. I *had* interfered in one of Will's murder investigations in the past, and almost got myself and Buddy killed for my efforts.

"But in this case, I have a lot more invested in this than the police do. To them, it's just another stalker case. To me, it's keeping me from being able to deliver a dog and get paid. And I need the money."

If I didn't collect my training fee for Lacy by the end of the month, I wouldn't be able to make my car payment. Nor would I have the funds to come see Jo Ann again in two weeks.

"Not to mention my concerns about my client's safety and sanity," I added.

"It sounds like Will *is* taking it seriously," Jo Ann said.

"Yeah, he is." I fell silent, trying to sort out a mild sense of disquiet about the whole dynamic between Will and me around this issue. "He blows hot and cold, when we're both investigating something. He did before, but that made more sense, because it was a murder investigation and I was butting in. But this is, *was* more my problem until I got that weird package, and Will came racing to the rescue, the big protector."

"And did you tell him not to come protect you?"

I felt my face heat up. I wasn't about to admit that I'd called him. "Well, no. I was kinda glad he was there." I also wasn't ready to get into how much this stalker scared me, with his ghost-like ability to strike right under one's nose.

But the threads of my thoughts regarding Will were starting to knit together. "It's that sometimes he acts like we're partners, and we're sharing information like equals. And then other times, he plays the 'I'm the sheriff' card and implies that I should butt out. Or sometimes flat out says to butt out."

"Marcia, I'm not sure it's fair to expect him to treat you as a partner when a criminal investigation is involved, even one that's important to you. He *is* the law enforcement officer, and you're not."

I tensed, huffed out air. "Whose side are you on?"

"Yours, but sometimes my job is to provide some reality testing. Putting myself in Will's shoes, I can see where it would be a struggle for him to know how to act under these circumstances. He's trying to respect your role in all this, your investment as you call it. But he's not used to being equal partners in an investigation. He's used to being the boss and assigning tasks to underlings."

"So you're saying I should cut him some slack."

"Exactly." Jo Ann sat back and smiled at me.

I rolled my shoulders. "Yeah, well hopefully he'll cut me some about going to see Joe Fleming."

If wishes were horses, beggars would ride, my mother liked to say.

My stable was definitely empty when I looked into Will Haines's steely eyes.

He gestured for me to come into his office. "Close the door."

I did so, then sat down in one of his visitor chairs. "We never firmed up about today. Do you have time for lunch?" I gave him a bright smile.

He didn't return it. "Marion County sent a deputy this morning to talk to Joseph Fleming. Seems he already knew about the stalking, because 'some woman,'" he made air quotes, "from the service dog people had been around asking him questions."

"I was careful. I took Buddy with me, and I asked Fleming to come outside. We walked around while we talked."

"I'm glad to hear that you took precautions, but you still interfered with an official investigation. Thanks to you, Fleming had plenty of time to come up with a good story."

Will was already using up a lot of his slack here. "And his story is that he never did anything to Rainey," I said in as calm a voice as I could muster, "and that he himself received some harassing calls."

His jaw tight, Will leaned forward in his chair. "Yeah. Look, Marcia–"

My own temper flared. So much for slack. "No, *you* look," I said through gritted teeth. "He didn't have time to think about his story when I showed up on his doorstep. And that is the same thing he told the Marion County deputy, isn't it?"

"Yes, but–"

"No, not *yes but*. I have a lot riding on this situation, while it's only one of many minor investigations to Marion County. And they probably wouldn't be investigating it at all if you weren't involved. You worked before in Albany, New York, which I'm guessing is about the size of Ocala. Tell me truthfully, did you all beat the bushes for every stalker some woman reported?"

"We took such reports very seriously."

I crossed my arms over my chest. "Uh huh, and what did you

do exactly?"

"We'd check their locks and suggest they get an alarm system, and tell them to be on the alert..." He trailed off and looked away.

"Put out a BOLO and file a report," I finished for him.

He picked up a pencil and punched its point against a pad of paper on his desk. The point broke. "And if they suspected a specific person, we'd go talk to that person."

"Yeah, and if he had a plausible story, what then?"

He turned his gaze back to me and made eye contact. The icy blue of a moment ago was now a dull gray. "Probably wait to see if anything more happened."

The weariness in his voice stuck a pin in my anger. I sank back in my chair.

He stood, walked around the desk and held out his hand. "Come on. I'll treat you to the Collinsville diner's blue-plate special."

A stubborn part of me didn't want to declare a truce just yet, but my stomach growled. And the diner's blue-plate special was almost always meatloaf. The best meatloaf on the planet.

I took his hand and let him pull me to a stand.

We kept the conversation light while we ate. It was past the height of the lunch hour, and we pretty much had the place to ourselves. Jane, the owner, had put the diner up for sale recently. She'd made one of her staff–my favorite waitress–the manager and had left town. Jane and I had never seen eye to eye, unless you counted glaring at each other. I was delighted she was gone.

I sopped up the last of the gravy on my plate with a roll. "So where do we go from here?"

Will startled. Anxiety flickered in his eyes. "What do you mean?"

I filed his body language away for later contemplation. "With the investigation into all this stuff that's been happening?"

He stiffened. "*We* don't go anywhere. I'll look into this Connors dude."

I bit back the snarky retort that popped into my mind.

Occasionally I could exercise impulse control. It was just spotty.

"And how will you go about looking into him?" I asked in as neutral a tone as I could muster.

"I'm going to go talk to him this evening."

I pushed my empty plate away. "I'm going with you."

"No, you're not."

"And why not? For one thing, it would be interesting to see how he reacts to me. Whether he seems to recognize me."

Will was quiet for a few seconds.

"You can't really think of a good reason why I shouldn't go, can you?"

"Yeah, I can, because you're a civilian."

"And you're going in your official capacity, outside of your jurisdiction?"

He went quiet again.

I leaned forward, arms crossed on the edge of the table. "Look, you did this during the Garrett case, first treating me like an equal and respecting my interest in the case, then closing me out and calling me a civilian. I got it then. You had a right to tell me to butt out of a murder case in your town that I was only tangentially involved in.

"But this is a case that is outside of your jurisdiction and personally involves me—my client, my dog, my best friend, my house. I don't see a single reason why we can't work as a team on this."

"Yeah, and you were being a team player when you went off half-cocked yesterday and talked to Joe Fleming?"

Okay, now he was really pissing me off. "You told me to get the guy's name, so I went to Ocala and confronted Rainey and got his name. Then I figured out how to find his current address, and I figured out a safe way to check him out."

His eyebrows shot up. "Safe?"

"Short of a Kevlar vest, I don't know what would have made me any safer?"

"Not going up to this guy's door to begin with, maybe?"

I wanted to point out that a female deputy would have done

the same thing in an investigation, and without an eighty-pound dog in tow. But this was getting us nowhere fast. I held up both hands, palms out. "You're out of your jurisdiction and I'm a civilian, so why can't we work as a team on this? I *like* it when you treat me as an equal."

He was staring at me, his cop mask in place.

"How about if I promise not to do anything without checking in with you first?"

"You're not going with me tonight, and that's final."

Grrr.

My goal was to jump up in indignation and stomp out of the diner, but sitting on a bench in a booth made that awkward. I had to scoot sideways to get out from under the table first. It took some of the impact out of my dramatic scene.

I stood at the end of the booth. "Fine. I'll go by myself. Right now!"

I turned and forced myself to walk at a normal pace out the door of the diner. Part of me wanted to flounce, but that was too drama-queenish. The angry part wanted to stomp.

And yet another part–the hurt part–wanted to bolt and find the nearest quiet spot to have a good cry.

I was pretty sure I'd just nailed the coffin lid shut on my relationship with Will Haines.

CHAPTER ELEVEN

I'd barely gone twenty feet down the sidewalk when a hand grabbed my elbow. I jumped and jerked away, then whirled around.

Will's jaw was clenched. He seemed to forcibly push the words out. "I'm sorry, Marcia."

My own jaw dropped. I quickly clamped it shut again.

"Let's go back to my office," Will said, "and I'll show you the info on Connors."

I fumed for most of the drive from Collinsville to Belleview.

In his office, Will hadn't really *shown* me the report on Connors, but rather had skimmed it in front of me, reading out loud the parts he deemed relevant. Nothing he'd said was news to me.

My fingers had itched to snatch the paper out of his hands, but I'd resisted the temptation.

Will had agreed, however, to take me with him this evening.

But first, I needed to pick up Lacy. As I neared Doc Murdock's clinic, I made myself take several deep breaths to calm down.

Doc's assistant, Sara, had Lacy ready to go. The dog was even sporting a perky little blue bandana. "We gave her a bath, on the house. She was pretty stinky. Doc says to keep her quiet and feed her chicken and rice for a couple days. Then she should be good to go."

I grinned at Sara. "Please, don't say the word *go* around her.

She's done more than enough going recently." I took the leash.
"I thank you for the bath, and so does my car."

"Oh, wait, Marcia," Sara called when I was halfway out the
door. She came over, carrying a clear baggie in her hand. "Doc
said to give this to you." She dropped her voice, even though
Joy, the receptionist, and the couple of other people in the waiting area were across the room from us. "This was stuck in her
fur. He thinks it was in her vomit and wasn't completely digested
before she got sick."

I wrinkled my nose and held the bag up to examine the contents—one of the soft round treats that I use.

Still keeping her voice down, Sara added, "He figured your
young man might want to get it analyzed, and he said to tell you
that he'll testify if need be."

I looked down at Lacy. Her dark eyes were watching me trust-
ingly, her white fluffy tail wagging.

Suddenly, I felt nauseous. "Tell Doc thanks for me."

The atmosphere was a bit tense in Will's car that evening. He
unbent a little when I gave him the baggie and Doc's message
about being willing to testify.

His expression grim, he said, "We gotta figure out who's
doing this first."

Then he'd reminded me, again, that I was to say nothing
while we were with Connors. I'd pointed out that he'd already
said that, three times.

We rode in stony silence. I looked out the side window at
the countryside whizzing by along Route 301. Occasionally we
would pass a gas station or convenience store.

I'd heard nothing back from the background check company.
Were they bogus?

"Did you find out anything interesting on Joe Fleming?" I
asked Will.

"Nope. He's clean as a whistle."

Somehow I wasn't surprised. He was either the nice guy he

seemed to be, or he was really good at fooling people and had stayed well under the radar.

Now I was wishing I'd used my free trial to find out more about Connors. The site hadn't said how much they charged for additional background checks, beyond the free one. But anything more than ten bucks was beyond my budget right now.

We arrived in Starke a little after six, usually a good time to catch people at home, and hopefully after they've eaten dinner, so they're not in a crabby mood.

Nonetheless, Sergeant Scott Connors was not a gracious host. He answered his apartment door in baggy gym shorts and a wife-beater undershirt that showed off his bulging shoulder muscles. When Will introduced himself, without mentioning me, Connors grudgingly let us in.

"The Marion County sheriff's already been here. I don't know nothin' about what's been happenin' with that crazy Bryant bi–"

Will shot him a sharp look that cut him off in mid epitaph.

"This is an informal little chat," Will said. "Just to follow up."

I was watching Connors' reaction to me. Basically, he had none. It was like I didn't exist.

I was tempted to pinch myself to make sure I wasn't dreaming this whole scenario. Maybe Will had refused to take me with him after all, and I was home in bed, sound asleep.

Will sat down on a lumpy maroon sofa that had seen better days. He looked up at me and pointed to the cushion next to him.

I was starting to do a slow burn. *Yeah dude, this is not how teamwork works.*

I sat and said nothing.

"Have you seen Lieutenant Bryant at all," Will asked, "since you were assigned to Camp Blanding?"

Connors perched on the arm of the stuffed chair across from us. "Naw, I didn't even know she lived in Florida. Not until that sheriff's deputy came around."

Dear Lord, I hope we're not giving this guy ideas he didn't already have.

I zoned out while Will asked him several questions that struck me as warm-ups. I was focused more on Connors' body language. He was working hard to appear nonchalant, but there was tension rippling beneath the surface. He looked as if he were resisting the urge to punch somebody or run from the room.

I was very glad I had not come to see him alone, although I would never, ever admit that to Will.

I tuned back into the words when Connors went off on a rant. "Army's been goin' downhill for years now, ever since they started lettin' girls in." His lip curled and he looked me in the eye for the first time.

I stared right back, not about to let him see me blink.

"All of a sudden, everybody's gotta be all politically correct. Pussy-footin' around." He held his hand up, fingers dangling down and danced them around in what I guessed was supposed to be people pussy-footing.

"And these girls act all tough, like they can take anythin' a man can, but then ya hit on one of 'em and all of a sudden they're screamin' rape."

"So that's all you did was hit on Lieutenant Bryant?" Will asked in a conversational tone.

"Yeah, and then she freaks out on me. Got me into a load of–"

Another sharp look from Will.

"Of crap," Connors said.

Will cocked his head to one side. "But you admitted to having sex with the lieutenant."

"Yeah." He turned to me again and licked his lips. "And she really liked it." His gaze flicked back to Will. "But then she turns on me, see?"

Pressure built in my chest. My stomach roiled. I so wanted to drive my fist right through this guy's face.

I struggled to keep my expression neutral. *How does Will do it?*

His face hadn't shifted one bit through all this. Total cop mask. He could've been discussing the weather.

"Tying her up, that was just part of having sex?" he asked.

"Yeah, it was the foreplay." Connors grinned, a man-to-man sly look in his eyes.

My hands clenched. I shoved them under my thighs. The soft sofa cushion offered little resistance.

"What kind of car do you drive, Mr. Connors?" Will asked.

"Sergeant Connors."

"Sorry." Will actually gave him a small smile. "Sergeant Connors."

"A white pick-up truck."

"You ever borrow a car from the motor pool at the base?"

"Yeah, sometimes, when I got Army business off base. Why?"

Will shrugged. "Just curious. You ever been down past Ocala on that Army business?"

Connors shook his head. "Had to go up to Jacksonville a couple a times."

Will nodded. "So you're not mad at Lieutenant Bryant for getting you in trouble?"

"Naw," Connors said too quickly. "'Cause after I told that captain, you know, the one that was investigatin' it. I told him yeah, we had sex, but I didn't force her or nothin'. Well, that was pretty much the end of it."

I clamped my teeth together and kept my eyes on Will's profile.

"Well, that about does it." Will stood. "Thanks for your time, Mr., uh, Sergeant Connors."

Connors had a smile pasted on his face. It didn't waver.

I pushed up from the sagging sofa. Will reached for my elbow.

Normally, I might have shrugged away from such a move, since I'm perfectly capable of standing up on my own. But something told me Will's gesture had another motive besides archaic chivalry.

He escorted me to the door, leaning forward to pull it open, then stepping back so I could go first. "Thanks again, Sergeant," he said over his shoulder and followed me out.

Again, he held my elbow as we walked out to the street.

"What's going on?" I asked in a low voice.

"Hang on 'til we're in the car." He opened the passenger door and closed it once I was settled in the seat, then went around to the driver's side.

He started the engine. "Just in case he is the one who came after you, I want him to know you're mine. Might make him think twice about messing with you again."

"*Just in case.* Does that mean you don't think he's Rainey's stalker?"

"Oh no, I think he is. But he didn't seem to recognize you."

"True. He didn't." I fumbled with my seatbelt, still a little shaky from the adrenaline my anger had produced. "I wanted to hit him so bad."

Will shot me a sideways glance. "You and me both."

"But you acted so normal."

"Lots of practice. See if you can find out when Rainey got the first harassing call."

I pulled out my phone and called her cell rather than the house number.

When Rainey answered she was whispering, but in a harsh tone. "What have you done, Marcia? The sheriff's people have been here, and my sister's furious."

I took a deep breath. After resisting the urge to deck Connors, I wasn't in the mood to deal with Sunny's hysterics over law enforcement. "Look, this guy spray-painted my house and tried to poison me, but he got my best friend instead. And he probably poisoned my dog. So in my book, it's a legal matter now."

No response, then snuffling noises. She was crying.

Sheez!

I took a deep breath. "I'm sorry." A conciliatory fib. "I didn't mean to snap at you. I've had a tense day. I called to find out when the stalking started. When did you first get the calls?"

"I told the deputy about that this morning."

Lord, give me strength.

"So tell me too."

"In January, shortly after Joe broke up with me. Did you talk to him?"

I ignored her question for now. "January," I repeated to Will.

"Who are you talking to?" Rainey said.

"Uh, my boyfriend." To Will I mouthed, *Should I warn her?* He nodded, his expression grim.

"Rainey, I don't want to freak you out but you need to know that Scott Connors is in Florida."

"What?" she yelped.

"Yeah, he's stationed at Camp Blanding."

"Oh no! Oh no!" Sobbing sounds.

"Rainey, calm down." My words seemed to have little effect.

"What doesn't fit," Will said beside me, "is that her sister said the guy running away was regular height and build. Connors isn't all that tall, but he's pretty beefy."

"What? Who's that?" Panic in Rainey's voice. "Who's with you?"

"It's my boyfriend," I repeated. "We're in his car. He's the sheriff of the next county south of us. He's unofficially helping the Marion County sheriff look into this."

You'd think having a law enforcement officer taking a personal interest would have been reassuring. But no, she freaked out even more. "Sunny's going to kill me! Can't you get him to leave it alone? Can't you get them all to leave us alone?"

I gritted my teeth. "No, because this isn't just about you anymore." It was one of those moments when I wished my mother hadn't drummed into me that cursing was a sin.

Maybe it was time for a change in tactics. "Hey, Lacy's home with me now. She seems to be doing okay. If she's stronger by tomorrow, I should be able to come down Wednesday and start up your training again."

"Oh, that would be so good," Rainey said.

I blew out pent-up air. The diversion had worked.

Rainey was babbling on. "Sunny says she's going to cook

stews for the dog. You know she's kind of a health nut, so she said no commercial food for Lacy, with all that artificial crap in it. When can Lacy stay with me?"

"Well, we'll see how things go, but maybe by next week."

"What?"

"Maybe sooner." I didn't want her to get started again. "We'll see. You know, not all people food is safe for dogs. I'll bring Sunny a list of what's good and what's not."

"That would be great. Thanks, Marcia."

I got off the phone quick, while she was calm.

"When did Connors get transferred to Camp Blanding?" I asked Will.

"Middle of December."

"Crapola."

"Yeah." His expression was grim. "I don't want you going there again until we're sure we've got this guy under control."

I frowned and stared straight ahead through the windshield. "Would you like to rephrase that, Sheriff Haines?"

A long pause. I caught movement in my peripheral vision—Will running his hand over his hair.

"I'd rather you didn't go to Rainey's without me," he said, his tone carefully neutral. "Can't you wait until the weekend to do more training? So I can go with you."

"Will, she's going to need at least ten more days, maybe longer because of this break." I heard the rising pitch of my voice, stopped, took a breath. "If I only go on weekends, that's five weeks. They'll be repossessing my car before I get paid for Lacy."

He gripped the steering wheel tighter but said nothing. After a moment, he glanced my way. "You're not going to leave Lacy with her, are you? What if this guy tries to get to the dog again?"

I sighed. "I don't know. I need to talk to Mattie. I'm not sure what's in the contract between Rainey and the agency. So what more can we do about this guy?"

"I'm going to compare notes with the Marion County sheriff, and ask him to beef up patrols around Rainey's house and in

Mayfair. If it's Connors doing this, maybe I've rattled him enough that he'll stop."

"Humph, he was tense, but he didn't seem all that rattled."

"That's 'cause he's good at not showing it, but he's afraid of authority."

"Why do you say that?"

"'Cause he was kissing up to me even after I insulted him by calling him mister instead of sergeant. And he shut down his cussing when I gave him a dirty look." He flicked his eyes toward me with a small grin. "How many drill sergeants do you know who don't, pardon the expression, cuss like sailors?"

I nodded. If the veterans I hung out with were any measure, cursing was part of everyday military language. "Now that you mention it, he did seem rather eager to please. And he certainly hasn't much respect for women."

I paused, rehashing the interview in my mind. "He didn't seem to recognize me, but maybe he never got close enough to see me that well. And he has access to all those lovely green cars in the Army motor pool."

"Yeah, but I don't think their license plates would start with a P," Will said. "I need to talk to your neighbor again."

"How and when will we know if Connors has been scared off?"

Will lifted the shoulder nearest me in a half shrug. "When nothing happens for a while."

"How long is 'a while?'"

He glanced over at me. "Long enough for you to get her trained and then get the heck out of Rainbow Bryant's life."

"Wait. Rainbow?"

"Yup, that's her proper name. You didn't know that?"

"No, I thought Rainey was a nickname for Lorraine."

Rainbow Bryant? My mind conjured up an image of the colorful plush doll I'd played with as a child.

I shook my head to clear it. "Hmm, Rainbow and Sunshine."

"Who's Sunshine?"

"Her sister. Goes by Sunny."

Will let out a bark of laughter. "Guess we know what their mother was smoking."

"Yeah, except there's an age gap between them, and Rainey said something about Sunny changing her name herself."

"Maybe their mother went on a hippie kick around the time Rainey was born, and the sister got sucked into it too. She would've been what, ten?"

"At least, maybe even in her teens." I sat back in my seat and stared out the window, although the scenery going by wasn't really registering. My mind was back on the issue of whether and when I would feel comfortable leaving Lacy at the Bryant home.

She was a sweet dog and had stolen a corner of my heart, despite my best efforts to stay detached. I couldn't in good conscience leave her in a dangerous situation.

Rainey seemed to think that the stalker would somehow magically be stopped by Lacy's presence, but I didn't see that happening. Whoever was doing this had seemed bound and determined to discourage me from finishing the training and delivering Lacy.

Maybe the stalker was Connors, and maybe Will had scared him off.

But how would we ever know that it was truly safe?

CHAPTER TWELVE

I'd silently forgiven Will his high-horse ways earlier in the evening, when he'd once again treated me as an equal partner on the drive home. So I gave it my best shot to get him to stay the night.

He stood close to me in my living room, heat radiating from his body. I felt lightheaded.

"You know I hate to leave." He stroked my cheek with his index finger.

Warmth spread down through my core.

He shook his head. "But I can't be two hours away from Collinsville when I'm short-staffed."

Much to my dismay, my eyes stung. "But it could be weeks now, before you can hire and train someone else."

He fingered a strand of hair that had come loose from my ponytail. My hair follicles tingled, as did other parts of my body.

I wrapped my arms around his neck. "You don't have to stay all night," I purred in his ear.

His body's enthusiasm for my suggestion was evident, but he groaned and disentangled himself from my arms. "Marcia, you're not making this easy."

I grinned up into his rugged face. "That's the idea."

He took both of my shoulders in his hands and held me away from him. "Sweetheart, do you really want our first time to be a quickie?"

I'd had trouble hearing the part after *Sweetheart*. I'd kind of melted at that word.

I dropped my forehead against his chest. "I can't take much more of this, Will. It's torture."

He lifted my chin with his index finger. "I'm going to schedule a couple of people this Sunday's day shift, even if it means paying overtime. Can you skip training with Rainey that day?"

"Yes," I said a little breathlessly, imagining an afternoon of delight.

"Good. I'll bring a friend who likes to paint. We'll be here about ten to get rid of that crap on the back of your house."

My mouth fell open. My heart fell to my toes. I swallowed hard. "Okay."

My body ached in certain places, which made me mildly ticked at Will, but other than that Tuesday was a nice, peaceful day.

Lacy was much improved. I took her and Buddy for a morning walk. As I'd hoped, I ran into Edna Mayfair. Benny and Bo romped around my dogs.

Since they were officially off duty, I let Lacy and Buddy sniff butts to their hearts' content.

Edna's attire of the day featured red hibiscus blooms against a green and black background. It was my favorite of her many muumuus. As usual, her hair stuck out in all directions.

How anyone could actually sign the motel's register after getting an eyeful of its proprietress was beyond me. But I knew that under that frazzled hair was a mind still sharp as a tack. She'd caught me, one time early on, eyeing her unusual garb and had cackled. "Honey, this is Florida, land of wear whatever ya darn well please."

Now she asked, "What've ya been up to, gal?"

I told her, in very general terms, about the stalking of one of my clients that had extended to attacks against me. "I hate to ask this of you, Edna, but I need you and Mrs. Wells to watch out for my house the next few days. I'm afraid this guy's gonna do something else." My voice caught a little. "I'm scared he'll do something to the dogs."

Edna patted my arm. "You know I'll help, sweetie. I'll set it up with Sherie. She and I can take turns keepin' an eye out."

"I'll talk to her about it," I said.

I needed to find out about the license plate anyway, since Mrs. Wells hadn't been home the previous afternoon when Will and I had knocked on her door.

I continued on down the road with the dogs. Lacy romped around with abandon amongst the palmettos and wild flowers along the shoulder. I concluded that she was fully recovered from her poisoning ordeal.

When we returned to the house, Mrs. Wells was standing on her porch next door. This was not an unusual occurrence. Despite having a large brood of her own, she seemed to have adopted me, and therefore felt it her duty to keep track of my comings and goings.

Sometimes this was annoying. Other times, like now, she was a godsend.

We exchanged greetings. Then I asked, "About the license plate on that green car. Was it a regular Florida plate, with the orange tree branch in the middle?"

She was silent for a moment. "I think it was a Florida one, but I'm not sure what kind."

I knew what she meant. Florida has a mind-boggling array of license plate options. "Did it have a white background?"

"Yes."

"What shade of green was the car?"

She frowned. "What's this all about, Marcia?"

I shook my head slightly. Will had coached me about not giving too much information up front that might influence her answers. "Dark green, medium or light?"

She crossed her arms over her crisp, white cotton shirt. "I guess more a medium green."

"Could it have been an Army staff car?"

"I thought they mostly drove jeeps."

I smiled a little. "I think that's just on TV. They have regular sedans too."

She lifted a hand to her face, tapped her index finger against her lips. "I guess it could've been."

I thanked her and told her about the need to keep an eye on my place the next few days. I knew darn well she would anyway. "Edna said she'd help."

Mrs. Wells nodded. "I'll give her a call and coordinate things."

"Thank you, ma'am. Oh, and Will's coming Sunday to help me get that paint off the house."

She nodded again. "He's a good man, Marcia."

I grinned. "Yes, he is."

I needed to get some training in with Jenny, but first I decided to call my "good man" and report my findings.

I told him Mrs. Wells's answers. "I guess it may or may not have been an Army vehicle she saw. What kind of license plates do they use?"

"Don't know," Will said. "I couldn't find anything online. Got a call in to the Camp Blanding's motor pool."

"So I was thinking," I grabbed a stray hunk of hair and twisted it around my finger, "maybe Buddy and I could come down one evening this week, for a few hours? I wouldn't be able to stay over, because of Jenny and Lacy, but…" I intentionally trailed off.

"Uh, I'm not sure. Let me get back to you on that."

I held the phone away from my face for a second and stared at it. I had thought he was as eager to consummate our relationship as I was, but he'd sounded downright tentative.

He doesn't want you anymore, a small voice in my head said. My counselor had dubbed it the Tiny Voice of Distrust.

I tried to ignore it as Will and I made small talk and then signed off.

I spent most of the rest of the day working with Jenny, and in the down moments, alternating between craving Will's body and being pissed at him for his reaction to my idea. Was his ardor already cooling?

Last night, his body had certainly been attracted to me, but was he rethinking his desire to have a relationship with me? I didn't mean to be a drama queen, but it did seem like chaos kept erupting in my life.

When I had finished with Jenny and she had crawled into her crate for a well-deserved snooze, I sat down at my kitchen table and called Becky's number. I got her voicemail. I left a breezy, just-checking-in message, the tone and content of which were fibs.

Desperate for some female commiseration, I called my mother. The problem here was that I had to dance around certain issues. I wouldn't say my mom is a prude, but she is a bit old-fashioned.

After the exchange of initial pleasantries and my obligatory inquiry into my brother's family's well-being, she asked, "What's up with your new beau?"

"Not much, I'm afraid."

I told my mother about our dilemma, or rather I danced around it, hoping she would get the idea. "He can't be too far from his town while he's understaffed, and I can't leave the dogs for all that long, so…"

"So you're not getting enough full-body contact," Mom said.

Again I found myself staring at the phone in my hand. "Okay, what closet have you stuffed my mother in? You let her out right now."

She chuckled. "Come on, Marcia. I may be a pastor's widow, but it *is* the twenty-first century, and you're hardly a virgin maiden."

Ain't that the truth, my pesky inner voice chimed in. I ignored it.

"I'm just afraid he'll lose interest."

"If he does, then it wasn't an enduring attraction to begin with. If two people are meant for each other, they'll go through a lot to stay together."

"And if they're not, they'll come apart all too easily, as I know full well from personal experience."

"Sweetheart," my mother's voice softened, "isn't it better to find out now if that's the case, rather than going further down the road with someone who isn't going to stick by you?"

I took a deep breath and let it out slowly. "I guess. But I kind of thought Will was the stick-by-me type."

"And he very well might be. It's too early to tell. But try to trust that whichever way things go, it will be for the best. Either you'll discover he's the fickle type..." She trailed off.

"Like my ex," I filled in for her.

"Or he'll be a keeper. You've got to give it some more time. You've only been dating what, two months?"

"Not even quite that," I said.

"So hang in there a bit longer and see what happens."

I was quiet, wondering how long *a bit longer* would be. I was so beyond horny, I could hardly sleep at night.

"Remember your father's favorite prayer?" Mom said.

"The Serenity Prayer."

"Exactly. You can only control your end of the relationship. You can't control the outcome. That's what you have to work on accepting."

I had been feeling better until she brought up that whole control thing. That had been the worst part of discovering that my ex was having an affair, the sense that my life was spinning out of control and I couldn't stop it.

But she was right. And hers was just a more religious version of the things Jo Ann Hamilton had been saying for a while. You can only control your own actions, not what others do.

Life is what happens while you're making other plans was another of Jo Ann's adages.

"Where would I be without you, Mom?"

She laughed. "A lot crazier than you already are."

I chuckled in spite of myself. "Gee, thanks!"

We said our goodbyes and I disconnected.

I did feel oddly comforted, even though I could have scripted both sides of most of that conversation. But it helped to hear someone else say it. Especially someone who had been happily married for four decades, before my father's death had parted them.

The next day, I made a snap decision to take Buddy with me. He was my mentor dog, I told myself. He'd helped me train Lacy with his examples of how to behave. Maybe he and I working together could also speed up the process of training Rainey to work with Lacy.

The reality was that I couldn't bear to lose him. If somebody was going to come do harm to my house, maybe burn it down, I didn't want my four-legged best friend trapped inside.

I felt bad about leaving Jenny there, but she would have been too much of a distraction. I prayed that Mrs. Wells and Edna's vigil over my place would be enough to discourage the stalker.

In Ocala, Rainey greeted me and the dogs with enthusiasm. Lacy seemed to remember her soon-to-be new owner, which I took as a good sign that she was bonding with Rainey.

I told Rainey about using Buddy to demonstrate how to work together with a service dog.

She accepted that as perfectly logical.

We worked in her backyard for a couple of hours. Rainey seemed more highly motivated to get things done. She knew she had to reach a certain level of comfort and proficiency before I would let Lacy stay with her. I was now seeing the side of her that made it through nursing school and Army basic training, not to mention two tours in field hospitals in Afghanistan.

When I called for a break, we were all hot and tired, but I was also quite satisfied with our progress. We went inside to get water for the dogs and cold drinks for ourselves.

Sunny greeted us with a deep frown. Her face was pale. "I didn't want to interrupt you. You all looked like you were getting so much done."

Rainey grabbed her hands. "What's happened?"

"Another call. Like the others, only more threatening."

Sunny's eyes were shiny. She looked down at Lacy. "He said he was going to kill your, quote, 'cute little service pup.'"

My stomach clenched.

Rainey went berserk. "That s.o.b.!" She threw Lacy's leash–which fortunately was no longer attached to the dog's service vest–across the kitchen. It bounced off the stove and fell to the floor.

Lacy, thinking her human was having an anxiety attack, put her paws up on Rainey's thighs and nudged her arm with her nose, reminding Rainey that she should pet her to ground herself and calm down.

Instead Rainey collapsed in a heap on the floor and threw her arms around Lacy's neck. She sobbed into the dog's white fur.

Buddy looked up at me and whined softly. I held out my hand and he touched it with his nose.

My heart ached for Rainey, but I didn't know what to say. My field was training dogs to help with past trauma that haunted our veterans in the present. I wasn't all that equipped to deal with current horrors.

Rainey's sobs subsided. She stared up at me from the floor. "What am I going to do?"

"You're going to keep training and wait for the authorities to find this guy and put him out of business." I wasn't real sure where those words had come from, but they sounded good.

We settled around the kitchen table with glasses of iced tea. The dogs sat at our feet, having quenched their thirst from the big bowl of water Sunny had put on the floor.

"As you might have gathered, I'm not fond of the police," Sunny said. "But in this case, I hope they can do their jobs and find this jerk."

I let the disparagement of law enforcement slide. "I hope so too."

We sipped our tea and munched on muffins that Sunny had once again produced. These were flavored with fresh strawberries.

"I've never had strawberry muffins before."

"I work with whatever's in season," Sunny said.

In my native Maryland, strawberries wouldn't be in season until June, but here in Florida they were a spring crop.

After our break, I told Rainey we were taking the dogs for a walk outside her yard. She cringed a little. I'm not sure why I thought this was the best approach. Maybe I was using the get-back-on-the-horse philosophy.

I fleetingly worried that the stalker might try to attack Lacy, as the anonymous call had threatened. But I doubted he would do anything blatantly aggressive while I was there.

He'd most likely wait until I had left Lacy with her new owner. No way could I do that now, not until he was caught. I pushed those thoughts away. That bridge didn't have to be crossed until we got the training done.

When I tuned back into my surroundings, I heard Sunny advising Rainey not to go out today. "This guy's probably watching, to see what your reaction is to his call." She shuddered. "He'll see you going out as open defiance and who knows what he'll do."

Rainey's eyes skittered from her sister's face to mine. She squared her shoulders. "I'm not letting him make me a prisoner in my house."

Sunny raised her clasped hands in front of her, almost prayer-like. "Please," she said in a choked voice, "I couldn't bare it if something happened to you."

I was waiting for Rainey to cave, but her eyes turned hard. Her jaw clenched, she said to me, "Let's do this!"

I barely managed to keep my own jaw from dropping open. That was not the response I'd expected.

I led the way through the living room, the dogs behind me, Rainey bringing up the rear.

Once outside, I said, "When you go out with Lacy, you'll have to deal with other dogs being walked and people who want to pet your service dog." I had already discussed with her how to deal with these situations. Now we would practice.

We started down the sidewalk in front of her house. "Remember the cover command?" I said.

Rainey nodded.

"When Lacy is in that position, if she perks her ears or wags her tail that means someone is approaching," I reminded her. "Move on ahead of us."

Rainey moved forward with Lacy.

I slowed and let her get about twenty feet out in front of me. "Okay, stop there."

Rainey stopped, and Lacy immediately turned back to face me.

As Buddy and I approached, Lacy's ears went up and her tail thumped. "See what she's telling you," I called out.

Rainey turned her head and smiled back at me.

I closed part of the distance between us. Then I unhooked Buddy's leash and twirled my finger in the air.

He ran up to Lacy and started barking excitedly and trying to sniff her.

Lacy thumped her tail again, once, but otherwise ignored him.

I jogged up to them. "Hi. What a pretty dog? May I pet her?"

Rainey had caught on. She turned a stony face toward me. "No, I'm sorry, but she's a service dog and she's working now." She tugged on Lacy's leash and walked away.

Buddy and I caught up with them again. I pointed out that she need not tug on the leash, just start walking and Lacy would follow. "But other than that, you did good."

Actually the stony expression was off-putting, but it wasn't my job to teach Rainey social skills.

Together, we walked around the corner onto an adjacent street.

A young man with blond hair was halfway down the block, his back to us, talking on his cell phone. He looked vaguely familiar.

Rainey turned her head toward me and opened her mouth. A loud crack rent the quiet suburban afternoon.

It took a fraction of a second for the sound's meaning to register. Heart pounding, I dove toward Buddy, covering his body with my own. We both collapsed to the ground.

A second crack.

I raised my head, frantically searching for the shooter. A glimpse of someone bolting around the fenced yard at the corner we'd just come from. A flash of red, a tanned leg in cutoff jeans, a white sneaker.

The shooter or someone running from the shots?

Jeans and a red jacket, echoed in my head. Maybe Rainey hadn't made that description up after all.

Heart in my throat, I looked around for her and Lacy, afraid to see one or both of them lying bleeding from gunshot wounds.

Rainey was crouched down ahead of me on the sidewalk, bending over Lacy in a protective stance.

Then she jumped up and bolted forward, the dog racing to keep pace.

"Get down!" I screamed.

She ignored me and kept running.

When she reached the body on the sidewalk, she looked back at me. Her face was slack with horror. "Help, Marcia! It's Joe!"

CHAPTER THIRTEEN

I whipped out my cell phone. "Shots fired," I yelled at the 911 operator. "Police and ambulance." I rattled off Rainey's address, surprised I could remember it under the circumstances. "We're around the corner from there."

Then I bolted forward to the blond-haired man on the ground. Rainey hovered over him. A red stain was rapidly spreading across his white tee shirt. His eyes were wide, unfocused, his skin pale.

"Rainey, I'm sorry…" he whispered.

I was shaking, totally freaked out. "We've got to stop the bleeding!"

That kicked Rainey into action. She tore open her shirt, buttons flying, and waded the cloth against Joe's wound. "Stay with me, baby," she pleaded as she picked up his wrist to take his pulse.

Joe looked up at her. "Love you…" His eyes rolled back in his head and he passed out.

She let his wrist drop and dug in her shorts pocket. "Get me a blanket and some pillows from the house." She tossed me a set of keys. "He may be going into shock."

Buddy and I took off back around the corner. Blood pounded in my ears. I felt sick to my stomach. I'd seen a lot in my day, but I'd never been shot at before.

I didn't like it.

Grateful for something to do, I bolted up the steps to the Bryants' front door. Fumbling for the right key, I finally got it unlocked.

Just over the threshold, I hesitated for a second, not totally comfortable with entering someone's house without them. "Sunny! There's been a shooting," I called out.

The only sound was the soft ticking of a clock somewhere. A faint odor tickled my nose.

I ran toward the stairs that led to Rainey's attic bedroom, Buddy hard on my heels. "Sunny, where are you?"

I grabbed a blanket and two pillows off of Rainey's bed and raced back the way I'd come. On my pass back through the kitchen, I saw the note, propped up against a pitcher of iced tea on the table.

R, RUNNING ERRANDS. BACK SOON. S

My brain belatedly registered the significance of the odor hanging in the air. I flashed back for a second to my college days and the dorms at the University of Maryland.

I bolted out of the house and ran faster than I thought possible all the way back to Rainey and Joe.

Sirens sounded in the distance. I prayed that was our ambulance coming.

Rainey instructed me to bunch the pillows under Joe's knees and feet. "Put the blanket over him."

I did as I was told, even though the temperature was in the eighties. As I spread the blanket over his arms, my hand touched his skin. It was clammy.

The sirens grew louder.

Rainey kept the pressure on Joe's shoulder, oblivious to the fact that she was only wearing a bra and shorts. Her lips were moving.

I suspected she was praying. Feeling a little awkward about it, since I don't check in with God regularly anymore, I silently joined her.

Two sheriff's department cruisers rounded the corner, the ambulance right behind. I blew out a sigh of relief.

A few seconds later, a paramedic gently nudged Rainey aside. He took over putting pressure on the wound.

A sheriff's deputy herded us over to his nearby car and opened both doors on the passenger side. My legs suddenly went wobbly on me. I sank down sideways on the edge of the backseat, the door hanging open. Buddy maneuvered between my knees and put his head on one thigh.

Rainey resisted getting into the car. Her gaze kept flitting to Joe's inert form and the paramedics working on him.

The deputy stood beside the car, asking us questions about what had happened. Despite the worried glances in Joe's direction, Rainey seemed calmer than I was. She, after all, was not new to gunfire and people bleeding.

Neither of our stories sounded all that coherent to me, but the deputy nodded and wrote things down on a small pad. Three other deputies were methodically checking the yards on either side of the street, their guns in their hands. Another cruiser rolled up and two more officers joined the search for the shooter.

"We've got him as stable as we can," one of the paramedics called over. "About to transport."

Rainey bolted around the deputy and raced over. She had dropped Lacy's leash, but the dog trotted behind her anyway. "I'm going with him."

"You related, ma'am?" the paramedic asked as he and his partner loaded Joe, now strapped to a gurney, into the ambulance.

"Yes. I'm his fiancée."

I stared at her.

"Okay, you can come but not the dog," the paramedic was saying as I climbed out of the cruiser and jogged over, Buddy in tow.

Rainey's determined expression morphed to panic. She began to shake. "She's a serv—"

I placed a hand on her arm. "There's no time to argue. Let them take him. You and I will follow in my car."

She nodded, then took off across the lawn of the house next to us, running along her neighbor's side of the fence that separated their properties. Lacy ran beside her.

The deputy huffed up next to me. "That isn't a great idea. The shooter could still be around here somewhere."

I doubted that was the case. He was probably long gone.

The deputy gestured toward his car. At my signal, Buddy jumped into the back. I climbed into the passenger seat, and the deputy drove us around the corner.

Rainey was on her porch, a tee shirt clutched in her hand, Lacy beside her. She hadn't washed her hands and there were bloodstains on the fresh shirt.

I doubted she cared.

"Sunny's not home, so the dogs have to go with us. I'm not leaving them here."

She wasn't getting an argument on that from me. I quickly loaded the dogs into the backseat of my car while she pulled on the tee shirt.

Joe had been whisked away, and we were sitting in the hospital ER's waiting area. The nurse on duty at the sign-in desk had only put up a token protest to the presence of the dogs.

Rainey had once again told the woman she was Joe's fiancée. I marveled at how easily the lie rolled off her tongue.

Personally I was a crappy liar, so it was just as well my mom had drummed into me that I shouldn't go there. I tried to follow that training, but I had been known to tell an occasional small fib. Okay, small to medium-sized fib.

I realized I was focusing on lying and maternal lessons to avoid thinking about the implications of someone shooting Joe Fleming. Had they been aiming at Rainey or Lacy? Or me, for that matter?

Or was Joe the intended target? Scott Connors wouldn't have any reason to go after him. Would he even know that Joe existed? Rainey and Joe had broken up before Connors was stationed in Florida.

Had Connors been keeping track of Rainey's life before he'd moved here? Had he requested the assignment to Camp Blanding in order to be close to her?

I could only hope that Rainey wasn't asking herself these same questions. She was already freaked out enough.

I couldn't put off consulting with Mattie any longer. I leaned over toward Rainey. "Will you be okay if I step outside for a minute? I need to make a phone call."

"Yeah." Her hand dropped to Lacy's ruff, the dried blood under her fingernails a morbid contrast to the dog's white fur.

I led Buddy out of the ER and stopped on the sidewalk. Digging out my phone, I called Mattie.

"Yes," she answered in her usual brusque way.

"Hey, this is Marcia, and I have a problem with the Bryant case." I filled her in as concisely as I could.

"Oh good heavens," she said when I had finished. Then she was quiet for a full minute. "I certainly can't ask you to keep working with her if it's dangerous. And Lacy could be harmed."

I knew Mattie well enough to know that the dog was her greater concern, even though she'd mentioned the danger to me first.

She sighed. "We might have to tell Ms. Bryant that we'll assign her another dog, once her stalker has been caught."

"She'll be heartbroken. She's already bonded pretty strongly to Lacy."

"I don't know what else we can do," Mattie said. "If you take her somewhere else to train, the stalker can follow her there from her house."

"Hm, maybe not. My boyfriend," I was finding it a little easier to say the word without stuttering, "he's in law enforcement. I bet he could take us somewhere without being followed."

"Okay, you can use my place. Let me know when you want to set it up. But you still can't leave Lacy with her until this is resolved."

"Well, this shooting today has brought us closer to solving the case."

"How so?"

"The guy who got shot was one of our suspects."

It dawned on me that I should have called Will. It wouldn't be good if he heard about the shooting from some other source.

I was about two minutes too late, but he didn't sound miffed, only worried.

"Just got off the phone with the Marion County sheriff. Are you and the dogs okay?"

It warmed my chest that he asked about the dogs as well as me. "Yeah. A little shaken up, but we're okay."

"So where are you?"

"At the hospital, with Rainey, waiting on news about Joe Fleming." I told him about Mattie's offer. "Can you get us there without being followed?"

"Of course I can." He sounded mildly insulted. "I also got a call from Mrs. Wells. The green car showed up in Mayfair about fifteen minutes ago. She said it could definitely be an Army car. When she came out on the porch, the guy turned around and sped away."

"It was definitely a guy?"

"No. I asked that. She said the driver had a baseball cap pulled down over their face and they were hunched down in the seat. And the license plate had mud on it."

I silently cursed TV shows and mystery novels that taught people how to commit crimes more effectively.

"I'll pick you up at eleven-fifteen tomorrow," Will said. "Tell Rainey we'll be there about noon. I'll have to drop you all at Mattie's in Belleview and then come back down to Collinsville for a few hours."

"That's a lot of driving for you. Why don't I take my car to Mattie's and you meet me there to go get Rainey. That way I can take her home when we're done and you don't have to come back."

"Okay. Be careful this evening, Marcia. I don't like it that this guy has moved on to bullets."

"You could come protect me," I said in my best sultry voice.

A beat of silence. "I wish I could, but not tonight. Too much happening."

What the heck did that mean?

"Just be sure to set your alarm," Will said.

I shook my head a little. My alarm was a gizmo made up of batteries, magnets attached to the door and doorframe, and a noisemaker that emitted an obnoxious screech when the connection between the magnets was broken. It was better than nothing, barely.

We signed off, and Buddy and I headed back inside.

A doctor in OR scrubs was standing in front of Rainey. I hurried over. He eyed Buddy but said nothing.

Rainey jumped up and threw her arms around me. "Joe's gonna be okay."

"We'll keep Mr. Fleming for a day, to make sure there's no infection," the doctor said to Rainey. "But he should be discharged day after tomorrow." He nodded to me and walked away.

"The folks here all bought the fiancée story?"

Rainey's cheeks turned pink. "Well, we did talk about getting married at one point."

I told her about the arrangements for the next day, to train at Mattie's place in Belleview.

Rainey chewed on her lower lip. "I guess I can do that, because you'll be there, and the dogs."

I had planned to leave Buddy home, since Will's car would be quite crowded otherwise. But the green sedan showing up in Mayfair today had me nervous. I opted to use Rainey's anxiety as an excuse. Having both dogs with us was more calming for her.

.

Will seemed excited when he met me and the dogs at Mattie's the next day, but his peck on my cheek was rather perfunctory.

"Guess who's AWOL," he said as he helped me load the dogs into his backseat.

I stopped in the middle of threading a seatbelt through Lacy's safety strap. "Scott Connors?"

"Yup, and he owns a .38, which is the caliber of bullet that went through Fleming's shoulder. But unfortunately, it hit a tree after that. It's too messed up to get a ballistics match."

I finished buckling Lacy in and stood up. "So they have the gun, but not Connors."

Would he take off without his gun? Maybe. Probably, if he owned more than one. That thought made me shudder.

"It may not be *the* gun. A .38 is a pretty common hand gun. But the Marion County sheriff has a BOLO out on him," Will said. "It's just a matter of time until they pick him up."

"So the sheriff's convinced he's the stalker?"

Will opened the passenger door for me. "No. The evidence is all circumstantial at this point. He's wanted for questioning."

Once Will had circled the car and dropped into the driver's seat, I asked, "Should Rainey get a restraining order against him?"

"I was going to suggest it."

"Can you tell her how all that works? She gets overwhelmed easily."

"Sure thing."

This time, Will pulled up right in front of Rainey's house. He stayed by the still-running car while I went to get her. That was one part so we didn't have to unstrap the dogs and then reattach their car restraints. But it was also to make sure the stalker didn't mess with the car.

Rainey froze for a second when Will stuck out his hand during my introduction. She finally shook it quickly, only offering the ends of three fingers.

"Do you want to ride in the back with the dogs, or up front?" I asked.

She opted for the backseat, as I'd suspected she would. It was crowded back there but she could pet Lacy to soothe herself and she didn't have to sit next to a strange man.

Will pulled away from the curb. He looked up in the rearview mirror. His lips thinned to a tight line at whatever he saw there, then he flicked his gaze back to the road.

I resisted the urge to turn around and look, assuming someone was following us.

But Will said, "Did something else happen, since yesterday?"

I glanced over my shoulder, then shifted around to face Rainey. Her skin had gone completely white.

"What happened?" I said.

Rainey waved a hand in a dismissive gesture. The effect was diminished by the fact that her hand was shaking. "Just another call. And I'm overreacting, like always." She twisted her face up into a look of disgust, apparently at herself.

"I don't think you're overreacting," I said. "I was shaking like a leaf all last evening, and jumped at every little sound outside."

I didn't mention that my reaction was as much about the green car showing up in Mayfair again as it was about the shooting. Will and I had discussed whether to tell Rainey about that. My opinion, that we shouldn't, had prevailed. She was already too close to the edge.

"What do these calls sound like?" Will asked.

I shot him a don't-keep-her-dwelling-on-the-topic look. He glanced my way and gave a slight shake of his head. I took that to mean that he hated to probe, but he needed the information.

"They're all distorted, mechanical," Rainey said. "Like the person's using something to change their voice."

"That's what Joe said about the calls he got," I blurted out.

"Calls? Joe got calls too?"

Dang! I hadn't told her about that either.

"Yeah. He said he there were three of them, telling him to stay away from you. I think it was shortly after you broke up."

"Which was when?" Will asked.

"Around last Thanksgiving," Rainey said.

Will and I exchanged a glance. I made a mental note to ask Joe when exactly the calls started.

"He wanted me to fly up north," Rainey was saying, "to spend the holiday with his parents. I had a meltdown at the mere thought, and we ended up in a shouting match. We were already having problems, about, you know, other things…"

I looked back over my shoulder. Her cheeks were flushed, and a tear trickled down one of them.

My chest ached for her. How cruel that her anxiety disorder was so limiting, and yet that was the nature of agoraphobia. The anxiety spread, becoming associated with more and more places and things. The thought of going someplace strange, of being trapped on an airplane, of meeting people who might judge her… I totally got her meltdown.

But then I had an advanced degree in psychology. Joe didn't.

And then there was the whole "other things" issue, the sexual problems that Rainey was convinced had really been behind the break-up. Joe had dismissed that, had seemed to understand the need not to push in that department. But sometimes what seemed like sexy seduction to a man felt like pressure to a woman, especially one with sexual trauma in her history.

"Hey," I said, "I thought we'd go see Joe at the hospital, after our training session today. My car's at Mattie's place."

Rainey's face brightened and she gave me a small smile. Lacy chose that moment to lick her chin. She chuckled in response to the doggy kiss, and I laughed too, more at the self-satisfied expression on Lacy's face. Dog and new owner were definitely bonding.

Mattie was pencil thin, with long, straight silver-gray hair, pulled back in a careless ponytail. No makeup adorned her leathery skin. Today, she sported jeans and a tie-dyed tee-shirt that reminded me of Sunny's wardrobe, only Mattie could more honestly claim the look. She truly had been a hippie in her youth.

Despite the unfamiliar location, the training session went well. Mattie left us to our own devices in her backyard, which was twice the size of mine. Part of it was taken up by brightly colored, doggie-sized playground equipment, or at least that's what it looked like.

Mattie also did obedience and agility training for regular dog owners and their canine companions. It was rather depressing that even the director of our organization didn't earn enough from training the service dogs to make ends meet. Or perhaps she chose not to draw a big salary so that more money could go toward helping the veterans get the dogs they needed. That would be like Mattie.

At one point during the session, my phone pinged. When it was time for a break, I checked for text messages. There was one from Will.

Call me asap. Good news.

He sounded a bit out of breath when he answered. "I can't talk long. Got things I need to do here. But I wanted to let you and Rainey know that we got him."

"Him who?" Muffled male voices and stomping sounds in the background. "Where are you?"

"Camp Blanding. And we got Connors. He came back here to get some stuff out of his locker. Turns out he has another gun, also a .38, and this one's been fired recently. The Marion sheriff thinks he has enough to hold him on attempted murder charges."

I actually jumped up and down a couple of times. My insides relaxed in places I hadn't realized were tense. "So he'll be in jail soon?"

"Either Marion County jail or the Army stockade. There's a little tug of war going on right now over jurisdiction, but either way he'll be out of circulation. And he had a note in his pocket. Let me see if I can remember the exact words. 'I never did nothing to that Bryant…woman.'"

Somehow I doubted Connors had used the word *woman*. More likely the b word.

"'And now she's gonna get me in trouble again. This *new* Army–new was in quotes–it su…stinks.'"

"Will, I can handle hearing bad words. I hang out with veterans, remember? I'm just programmed not to say them myself."

"And I like that about you. You're…ladylike."

I snorted. "Come again?"

"Okay, maybe not the right word. Anyway, Connors's note went on a bit more about how the Army isn't the he-man place it had once been, along the lines of his rant the other night. I suspect he was going to leave the note in his locker as a not-so-fond farewell."

"Hey," I said, "does this mean she doesn't need a restraining order?"

We'd never gotten around to discussing that with Rainey earlier. She'd already seemed too uptight to get into the topic.

Now I glanced over at her. She'd been following my end of the conversation, a big smile spreading across her face. Her eyes had gone wide at the mention of restraining orders.

"No, you don't need one," I told her. "They've caught Connors."

"I'll keep you posted," Will said in my ear. "Gotta run."

"Okay, thanks for letting us know."

My heart swelled as I disconnected. This man really was a good guy.

Rainey had obviously been struggling to contain herself. Now that I was off the phone, she threw her arms around me. "Is it over?"

"Probably," I said. I didn't want to give her false hope. I suspected more evidence would be needed to convict Connors of stalking, much less shooting Joe.

Had Joe gotten a look at his assailant? I suspected not, or Will would have said so.

We had brought our own refreshments, so as not to impose on Mattie. We settled around her picnic table under the shade of a live oak tree. I opened a bottle of water for the dogs and poured it into my collapsible dog dish. Buddy politely waited while Lacy drank her fill.

I grinned down at him. "You're such a gentleman."

"I've got muffins." Rainey held up a paper bag. "Raisin bran this time."

I mock groaned. "Hanging around your sister is dangerous."

Rainey gave me a strange look.

I picked up one of the muffins she had set on the table and

pretended to slap it against my right hip.

Light dawned on her face and she laughed.

"My pants are getting tight." It was only a slight exaggeration. All excess calories automatically gravitate to my already abundant hips.

We munched on the muffins and sipped iced tea from two thermoses, one sweet tea, one barely sweetened.

She used her finger to smush some crumbs on the muffin wrapper and carry them to her mouth. Without looking up, she said, "I have a confession to make, if you promise not to tell anyone."

Suddenly I had a bad feeling, and I wasn't willing to make that promise.

Her head came up. "Please, Marcia, I can't go to jail. I'd never last a day."

"What are you talking about?" It came out a little harsher than I'd intended.

She gazed down at the table again. "Your friend Becky. I was the one who doctored her drink."

My mouth fell open. I remembered that persistent niggling feeling I'd had one day after leaving Rainey's house. Was that the day she'd said something about Becky being sick? Now that I thought about it, I was pretty sure I'd never told her or Sunny the name of the sick friend I'd been tending.

Anger flared in my chest. "So you've been doing *all* of this crap?" Resisting the urge to grab her and shake her, I clenched the thermos in my hand until my knuckles turned white.

"No, no." She held her hands up, palms toward me, as if to ward off my anger. "Only that one thing. All the rest of it has been the stalker." She dropped her hands and plucked at the muffin wrapper. "You see, I get these crushes on people, male and female. My counselor says it's my inner child, trying desperately to find a parent who will love her."

I'd never given the inner child therapeutic model much thought before. It had become such a cliché in our society. But after knowing Rainey–and seeing her inner child come out and take over more than once–maybe the model had merit.

"I heard you that day on the phone," she said, "making dinner plans with her, and I just got really mad."

I know the feeling, lady!

I clenched my teeth shut for a moment, to keep from yelling at her. Once I had my anger somewhat reined in, I said, "How come you could follow me to Belleview but you can't do other things on your own?"

"If I'm mad enough, it overpowers the anxiety for a while. Afterwards…" She dropped her gaze to the table. "I was shaking so hard I could hardly drive on the way home."

I had a whole lot of trouble feeling sorry for her about that.

"I talked it out with my counselor." She waved a hand in the air as if waving away a gnat. "She helped me get over my crush on you, so it's okay now."

The nonchalance of her tone pissed me off even more. Because of some crazy crush she had, my best friend spent a day of her life puking her brains out.

Again, I reined my temper in. She was confessing, and apologizing in her own limited way. Blowing up at her would only complicate the training that still needed to happen. I just wanted to get it done and get this woman out of my life!

When I was sure I had control over my voice, I said, "But why did you send me the paper towels?"

"Paper towels? What do you mean?"

"The ones she and I used to sop up the tea the waitress spilled on her."

"Oh, yeah, I owe her an apology for that too. I intentionally bumped into the waitress."

I shook my head a little. This conversation was answering some questions and confusing the issue at the same time. "I got a box full of used paper towels, with brown tea stains on them, in the mail a couple of days later."

She cocked her head to one side. "That's weird."

"Wait, of course you didn't send them. There was a note on one of them, warning me to stay away from Ocala."

Rainey shuddered. Lacy, who had been lying at her feet, sat up and put her head in Rainey's lap.

Despite the seriousness of the situation, I was pleased to see Lacy so responsive to the shifts in her owner's mood. I resisted the temptation to say *Good girl*. Praise and treats should come from Rainey now.

"That means the stalker followed me when I followed you." Rainey's voice shook.

And followed us to the restroom. He was probably listening outside the door.

I stood up abruptly. "Come on, let's get back to work." I needed something to distract myself from the creepy chill running down my spine.

CHAPTER FOURTEEN

At the reception desk at the hospital, we were told that Mr. Fleming was awake and allowed to have visitors. The nurse looked askance at Buddy and Lacy. "I know they're service dogs, but his roommate's recovering from surgery. He may not appreciate a parade of people and animals coming through."

I turned to Rainey. "Can you consider this part of your training? We'll walk you and Lacy as far as the elevator and you go on from there."

Rainey nodded. "I think I can do that."

"Are cell phones okay?" I asked the nurse.

"Of course. We use them ourselves now to communicate with each other on the floors."

"Call me," I said to Rainey, "if it's feeling like too much, and I'll come get you."

The nurse smiled at her. "Mr. Fleming's room is on the second floor, two doors down from the elevator, on the right."

Rainey nodded again and we headed for the elevator. Fortunately, it was empty, which would make it easier for her. With only minimal hesitation, she led Lacy in.

After the doors closed, Buddy and I settled into a small sitting area near the front entrance to wait, me on one of the uncomfortable beige chairs and Buddy sitting at my left knee.

I hadn't thought to bring my ereader so I picked up a magazine. I'd been leafing through it for a couple of minutes when Buddy's tail thumped, the signal that someone was approaching.

I looked up. A man and a boy had entered the sitting area.

"Is it okay if he pets your dog?" the man said.

I smiled at them. "Thank you for asking, and unfortunately I have to say no."

The little boy's face fell. He gave his father a confused look.

"Is he aggressive or something?" the father asked.

"No." I pointed to Buddy's red service dog vest. Then I leaned forward, realizing this could be a teachable moment. "What's your name?" I asked the boy, who looked to be about five.

"Freddy."

"Okay, Freddy, when your Dad goes to work, are you allowed to call him whenever you want and pester him while he's working?"

The boy looked confused again. "I don't call him at all, but Mommy does sometimes."

The father crouched down beside his son. "But she only calls me if it's something important."

I thanked the universe for the fact that the man was a quick study.

"Right," I said. "So you see, Freddy, this dog is working right now, and he can't be distracted while he's working. These words right here." I pointed to Buddy's vest again. "They say 'service dog' and that means he's working."

"Are the vests always red?" the dad asked. He straightened up and took the seat two chairs over.

"No, sometimes they're blue or black. They can be any color really, and they may say 'guide dog' or 'assistance dog.'"

"A sister dog?" Freddy said.

His dad and I chuckled.

"Assistance," I said, enunciating more clearly. "It means *helper*. The dog is helping the person he or she is with."

Little Freddy's face brightened. "I've got a sister."

"That's why we're here," the dad said, "to see his mom and new baby sister. But we came at a bad moment. The nurse said my wife's taking a shower."

I tried to hide the shudder that ran through me. I could only imagine how difficult it would be to do something even as mundane as showering after just having had a baby. Little Freddy seemed to be okay, but in general, I'm not fond of rug rats. I'd be very glad to leave my childbearing years behind me, so my mom would stop bugging me for more grandchildren.

I glanced over at the little boy. He was staring longingly at Buddy.

"I'll tell you what," I said. "I'm going to give him the signal that he's off duty. Then he won't be working anymore and you can pet him."

Freddy reached toward the dog.

I held my hand up. "Wait. Watch this." I cross my wrists, uncrossed them, then crossed them again. Buddy stood up and wagged his tail. "Now it's like when your Dad comes home. He's not working anymore and you can distract him."

The man grinned at me over his son's head, as Freddy stroked Buddy's fur.

The dog's tail beat a steady rhythm against the leg of my chair.

The soft whir of elevator doors opening. I glanced over. Rainey and Lacy were headed our way.

"Freddy, this white dog coming toward us, she's working now too, so don't try to pet her, okay?"

Freddy nodded, a solemn expression on his face.

Rainey glanced nervously at the dad as she approached. I stood up and held my hand out palm down toward Buddy. He touched my palm with his nose. "And now my dog is working again as well."

Freddy stepped back and wrapped an arm around his dad's knee. He looked like he really wanted to stick his thumb in his mouth. My heart melted a little.

"Rainey," I said, "this is Freddy and his dad. They're here to visit Freddy's mom who just had a baby girl."

Rainey visibly relaxed. "Nice to meet you Freddy and Freddy's dad."

The man stood up. "Bob Hudson." He extended his right hand.

Hopefully her hesitation was only obvious to me. She took his fingers and gave them a quick shake.

Then she turned to me. "Joe wants to talk to you. Says he wants to thank you personally for helping yesterday."

"I didn't do all that much."

"He was pretty insistent. He seems to be doing okay. They're going to discharge him tomorrow morning."

"Okay. You want to keep Buddy with you here?"

"Sure."

I smiled down at Freddy. "I'm going to release him again so you can pet him, but you can't pet the white dog, okay?"

Freddy nodded silently.

I gave Buddy the off-duty signal, then handed his leash to Rainey.

"Good luck with the new baby," I said to Mr. Hudson.

"Thanks." Then *sotto voice*, he added, "We're gonna have our hands full for a while."

Another tremor ran through me. I maintained my smile with effort.

I found Joe's room without any trouble and knocked softly on the half open door.

"Come in."

I complied. Joe was in the bed closest to the door. A white curtain was pulled across the middle of the room.

"Hey, Marcia." Joe's face brightened. He tried to push himself more upright and winced. After fumbling with a remote control, the head of his bed rose. His left arm was inside his hospital gown, white bandages peeking out of the neck opening.

"I have to tell you something fast, 'cause the nurse just gave me a pain pill and they tend to knock me out. I didn't want Rainey to know this. It would freak her out. But I started getting those calls again."

My stomach clenched. "Really? When?"

"About three days ago, and then another one yesterday morning. Same distorted voice telling me to keep away from Rainey."

"Did you tell the sheriff about them?"

"No. I didn't think they were related to me getting shot, not until Rainey told me she'd also gotten a call yesterday."

"Actually her sister took the call, but that was bad enough. It shook Rainey up, and then... I guess you didn't see who shot you?"

"Nope. No clue. When I first woke up and they told me I'd been shot, I thought it was something random, like somebody cleaning their gun and not realizing it was loaded. I didn't connect it to Rainey at all. I wasn't even on her block then."

"But you were nearby, and you were on your phone. Who were you talking to?"

He shook his head. "It had just rung, and the number was blocked. I answered it and then boom."

"Did you tell the sheriff that?"

He shook his head again. "I didn't even remember it until now, because you asked about it."

"Okay. I'll pass all this along to law enforcement. What were you doing there anyway?"

He shrugged his good shoulder and winced a little. "Just walking around."

I stared at him, silent.

"I was trying to get up the nerve to knock on Rainey's door. I've been... worried about her."

That sounded plausible enough.

But he could also be the stalker, and the shooting was indeed a random coincidence. He could've been hanging around Rainey's neighborhood, looking for an opening to terrorize her again.

"So how are you doing?" I asked belatedly.

"I'm fine. I only wish they hadn't gotten me in my left shoulder."

"Why?"

"I'm left-handed."

My brain had a funny little reaction to that piece of information. But I couldn't figure out what it was about.

Joe's body was starting to droop, along with his eyelids. I gently took the remote gizmo out of his right hand and found the button to lower the bed.

"Thanks," he mumbled.

"Take care." As I turned to leave, I came face to face with Carrie Williams.

She held a terra cotta planter with green ferns and philodendron in one hand and the string of a huge smiley face balloon in the other.

Her toothy smile faltered at the sight of me.

"Hi, Carrie." I eyed her too tight black suit that accentuated her curves. She must have come directly from wherever she worked. "Uh, Joe's a little sleepy now. The nurse gave him a pain killer."

"What are you doing here?" she demanded.

I literally took a step back. "I could ask the same thing."

So much for giving her the benefit of the doubt.

She lifted her perfect nose in the air and nudged forward.

I took the high road and moved aside, swinging my arm in a come-on-in gesture.

She swept past me, leaving a trail of some fruity fragrance. The balloon bopped me in the head.

I stepped out into the corridor to the sound of her syrupy voice asking how "her little Joey" was doing and Joe's indistinct reply.

I mimicked sticking my fingers down my throat and made retching noises. Fortunately or unfortunately, I'm not sure which, she didn't seem to hear me.

Before returning to Rainey and the dogs, I found a secluded corner where I could call Will. I relayed what Joe had said.

Again, I had one of my dang niggling feelings, but I couldn't lasso the thought and bring it out into the light of day.

"Okay," Will said, "I'll pass all that on. Connors has confessed to making the early calls to Rainey, but insists he hasn't done anything in months, and that he never did more than call her."

I sat down on a small backless bench and leaned against the wall. It had been a long day. "Did he say anything about calling Joe, then or lately?"

"No, I don't think so."

"Do you think Connors is telling the truth?"

"Heck no. I think he did all of it. But he knows they can get his phone records, so I'm guessing he figures if he confesses to the calls, he'll sound more convincing when he swears that's all he did. Oh, more good news. The Army won the tussle over jurisdiction, but they're holding Connors without bail since he's an obvious flight risk."

"Hallelujah! Can I tell Rainey that?"

"Of course."

"I miss you," I said.

A half beat of silence on the other end of the phone. "You saw me this morning."

"Yeah, but I wouldn't call that quality time. You free tonight? I could come down for a couple of hours." I was dog tired, but I'd find the energy somehow if it meant I would finally get to do the hokey-pokey, as Jo Ann called it.

"Afraid not. Another commissioners' meeting."

"What? Isn't that the third one this month?"

"I don't know. I stopped counting."

His voice sounded appropriately aggrieved, but I couldn't help wondering if he was looking for an excuse not to get together.

Stop that!

"Okay, well, I guess we won't need to train at Mattie's tomorrow. So I'll see you Sunday?"

"Yeah, see you then."

I disconnected and blinked back tears. No date this weekend, except to paint my house.

You've blown it, Banks. He's backpedaling.

"Aw shut up," I told my inner voice.

I should have been ecstatic as I drove home from Rainey's. She certainly had been when I'd told her that her stalker was in Camp Blanding's stockade with no shot at bail. And now I could finish her training and get paid for Lacy, thus being able to make my car payment.

But instead of being happy, I was in a foul mood, thanks to Will. And the niggling feeling that I was missing something wasn't helping. I was getting rather annoyed with that feeling. Why couldn't my brain just spit things out instead of playing games with me?

I was ten minutes from home when it hit me. I bopped myself on the forehead with the heel of my hand.

I no longer had the paper towel with the note on it to confirm my suspicions.

And by the way, why hadn't Will informed me about any fingerprints they'd found on the box? Or the analysis of the treat Doc Murdock had given me?

As soon as I was home, I dumped my purse on the sofa and bolted out into the backyard.

As I'd thought, the red letters painted on my house were slanted to the left. The way a left-handed person would most likely make them.

CHAPTER FIFTEEN

I called Will, but it went straight to voicemail. It was dinner-time. His stupid meeting couldn't have started already, could it? I texted him.

Graffiti letters slanted left. Joe left handed.

Didn't shoot himself, he texted back.

I know. I wasn't going to debate that coincidences did happen via texting. *Connors left handed?*

I'll check.

Miss u.

Me too. Gotta go.

I stuffed my phone back in my pocket, totally frustrated. My body ached.

I'd been better off before I'd ever met Will Haines. My sexuality had gone dormant after three years of post-divorce celibacy.

And that dang niggling feeling was still there. What else had I missed? I strained my brain for a few minutes, with no results other than a slight headache.

I opted to distract myself from my unhappy body by doing a short training session with Jenny. We practiced the cover command. She was now consistently turning back and facing the way we'd just come every time I stopped walking.

Next, I needed to add the last part, the alert signal—ears perked, one tail wag—that she would give her owner if someone was approaching from behind. But for that I would need Becky or Will's help, so it would have to wait for another day.

By Saturday afternoon, Rainey and Lacy were doing so well as a team that I decided to leave Lacy with her.

"This way," I said to her and Sunny, "you all can start to get into a routine around the house, and I'll be back Monday for more training."

Rainey's face split with a big smile. She literally jumped up and down.

I held up my hand. "Keep in mind that it's fine to play with her when she's off duty, but she is not a pet. No spoiling her. And be sure you're clear in your signals about when she is and is not on duty."

We had worked out a new release signal, raising the left arm in the air and tapping that elbow with the right hand.

Rainey nodded, still grinning from ear to ear, and gave Lacy that signal now. Then she plopped down on the kitchen floor next to the dog and rubbed her head with enthusiasm. Lacy licked her new human's face.

Warmth spread through my chest. I glanced across the kitchen at Sunny.

Her stringy hair hung forward, partially shielding her face, as she looked down at her sister and the dog. From what I could see of her expression, it was neutral. Her arms were crossed over her chest.

She raised her head, made eye contact, and her posture relaxed. She gave me a small smile. "Finally this day has come." She dropped her arms and rubbed her palms against her jeans-clad thighs. "Guess I'd better start on some stew for this sweet girl."

"Keep in mind that list I gave you," I said. "And check with me before you add anything other than what's on the okay list. You'd be surprised at the things that are good for humans but can harm dogs."

Sunny nodded. "Don't worry, we'll take good care of her. She's a member of our family now. Right, Rainey?"

Rainey looked up from the floor, happy tears pooling in her

eyes. She nodded and threw her arms around Lacy's neck.

I grinned at all of them, my chest swelling with a sense of pride over a job well done. For now, that feeling was compensating for the small ache in my heart at the thought of parting permanently with Lacy soon.

Once I was outside of Ocala, pointed south on I-75, I called Will and told him the good news. "Are you free this evening? I feel like celebrating."

"Sorry, 'fraid not. Hey, I've got some good news of my own. I've got two interviews lined up with potential deputies."

"Good, then maybe things will go back to normal soon."

A soft chuckle from Will. "I thought crazy and chaotic *was* normal for you. It's mostly what I've witnessed so far."

For some reason, that comment grated, but I faked a cheery tone. "Say, you never told me if they found any fingerprints on that box or the paper towels inside."

"Not on the towels, which isn't surprising. They're too rough. Also only a few prints on the outside of the box, which is kind of curious."

"How so?"

"Mailed boxes get handled by a whole bunch of folks, and that box looked like it had been around for a while. This was probably its fifth or sixth journey through the U.S. Postal Service."

"So it should have had tons of prints then."

"Exactly. Anyway, most of the ones that did come up weren't in the system, but there was one that was very interesting. It was pretty clear, on the sticky side of the tape closing the box."

A pause.

"Don't keep me in suspense. Did it come up in the system?"

"Yeah, for a dead woman."

"Say what?" I pulled over on the shoulder. This conversation had gotten a tad too intriguing to go hand in hand with driving a car.

"She committed suicide after killing somebody in a hit and

run accident. She jumped off the Golden Gate Bridge."

"So how the heck did her print get on that tape?"

"Good question. There may be a simple answer, like she was one of the ones that used the box previously, and the sender reused the same tape."

"Who reuses the same tape?" I said. "It doesn't usually have enough sticky left."

"Do you recall if the box top was shut tight, or was it at all loose?"

"I don't remember. It couldn't have been too loose though, or I would've noticed."

"Yeah, probably," Will said. "Well, we may never know what that's about."

"You're pretty blasé about it."

"Hey, that's police work. You have stuff come up sometimes that doesn't make any sense. And you don't always get all the answers to your questions."

A pick-up truck blasted past me, reminding me of Will's comment about inattentive drivers hitting cars that were stopped on the shoulder. I shifted my car back into gear and pulled into an opening in the traffic.

"I take it Connors' prints weren't on the box," I said into the phone.

"No, but he could've been the one who wiped it down and then sent it through the system."

"Where it collected the few prints that it did have."

"Yup."

"Hey," I said, "did the lab analyze the treat in the baggie yet?"

"Afraid not. We don't have a crime lab so I gave it to the Marion County sheriff. I'll call Monday and see if he's heard anything. The sample they took from my backseat came back negative for any toxins."

"Did they test it for chocolate?"

"I mentioned that to the deputies that night, but they might or might not have passed on those instructions to the lab. I'll check on that on Monday too."

"Okay."

I'd tried to keep the frustration out of my voice. It would be helpful to know if Lacy was indeed intentionally poisoned. But Marion was a big county. Examining dog treats probably wasn't a high priority at their crime lab.

"Anything interesting in Connors's or Fleming's phone records?"

"Connors made four calls to Rainey's home number in January and early February. After that nothing."

"So he could be telling the truth, and that's all he did. Maybe somebody else got ideas from those calls." Carrie Williams' face popped up in my mind's eye.

I shook my head. Just because I didn't like the woman much didn't mean she was a stalker.

"Or he got smart after that," Will said, "and started using a throwaway cell phone."

"What about Joe's records?"

"Marion County Sheriff couldn't get a subpoena for them, not enough probable cause."

I blew out air.

"Gotta go," Will said. "I'll see you tomorrow about ten-thirty, okay? Don't worry about getting paint or anything. I've got it covered."

"Thanks, that's really sweet."

I realized I was listening to dead air. Will had already disconnected.

Becky was the first to arrive the next day. I stifled a laugh at her idea of painting attire–denim short-shorts and a peach halter top that left little to one's imagination. Her dark curls were mostly covered by a flowered-print kerchief in shades of peach and blue.

She was lugging two plastic gallon jugs of dark liquid.

I raised an eyebrow at her. "Store-bought iced tea?"

"Of course not. I repurposed the old jugs." She hefted them

onto the bistro table on my deck.

"Speaking of jugs, don't you think that top's a little revealing?" I was dressed in an old long-sleeved shirt and my funkiest blue jeans.

Becky put her hands on her hips. "Don't judge."

"I'm not judging. I'm worried. I don't want the guys falling off the ladder because they get distracted when you walk by."

She smirked. "You're just envious."

My mind flashed to Carrie Williams. I faked a chuckle. "That, my dear friend, is a given when I'm around you."

Her expression shifted to something unreadable. "So how are you and Will doing?"

"Oh, same old, same old. Still struggling to find time together, what with the distance and him being short-handed."

"In other words, you haven't done it yet."

I sighed. "No, but I'm hoping my life can get back into some kind of routine now. I'm within a few days of finishing up with this client." I told her about the stalker being caught.

Becky's face brightened. "Hey, that's great news. Did he admit to spiking my iced tea?"

"No, only to the earliest calls to the client."

I opted not to tell her that my client had done the tea spiking. It was too complicated to explain, and frankly not all that believable unless one knew Rainey. I flashed back to Jo Ann Hamilton's diagnosis of borderline personality disorder.

I'd read up on it after that session. The crushes and the tea spiking definitely fit with that disorder.

"Connors didn't even admit to all the other stuff he did to the client," I said. "But Will sounded pretty confident that the Army wouldn't be letting him loose anytime soon."

And as if I'd conjured him up, Will came through the gate, lugging a six-pack of beer in one hand and two gallons of paint in the other.

A wiry young man of about thirty followed him. Paint rollers stuck out of the top of the plastic bag he carried. Two large bottles of Gatorade were tucked under his other arm. His dark curly hair was short, his eyes chocolate brown, his skin a light bronze.

Will put his burdens down on the edge of the deck. "This is Andy." He leaned toward me and said *sotte voice*, "Be nice to him. I don't want him to quit too."

"Hey, boss," Andrew said, white teeth flashing, "about that raise?" He deposited the bag and Gatorade on the deck and stuck out his hand. "Andy Matthews. You must be Marcia."

I already liked the guy. He'd pronounced my name correctly.

I grinned and shook his hand. "How'd you know which of us was which?"

"Will said he was dating a gorgeous redhead."

I snorted and gestured toward Becky. "This is my friend, Becky."

Andy's eyes went wide. "Uh, how do ya do, ma'am?" He stumbled a little over the words.

Becky extended her hand with a flirty smile. "I do good, Andy. Pleased to meet you."

Will was all about getting the painting done before the sun heated things up to an unbearable level, so we got down to work. I had an extension ladder and Will had brought one too. The guys started at the top of the wall, one on each end, slapping a layer of primer over the red paint so it wouldn't bleed through the top coat.

Meanwhile Becky and I painted the lower part of the wall– below the graffiti–with the top coat. Will hadn't been able to match the white paint of my house exactly–it's amazing how many variations of white there are. But once the whole wall was done, it would be close enough to the shade of white on the adjacent walls.

We took a break at twelve-thirty to eat some lunch. I had made sandwiches–sprouts and cheese on whole grain for Becky, the vegetarian, and tuna salad for the rest of us. We brought kitchen chairs out onto the deck and sat around the wobbly bistro table. The sun had moved over the peak of the house and the deck was now in the shade.

Becky and Andy chatted away as if we weren't even there. Will caught my eye and winked. We kept quiet, munching on our sandwiches.

Becky was always animated, but today she seemed to come to life in a whole new way. I'd heard plenty about her dating escapades but I'd never seen her in action before.

Andy had been a little stiff with her at first, self-conscious I assumed. But Becky knew just how to put a man at ease.

Once the sandwiches were history, Will pushed himself to a stand. "Let's get back to it."

Becky wrinkled her nose at him. "You're a slave driver."

Will grinned and cracked an imaginary whip. "This young man's covering the night shift. I gotta get him home in time for a nap before he goes on duty tonight. Can't have Collins County's finest falling asleep in their squad cars."

I pasted on a smile but my heart had sunk to my toes. I'd hoped Will would stay for at least a little while after the others left.

The primer had already dried, and the guys made quick work of the top coat. There wasn't much for Becky or me to do except hold the paint buckets for them when they had to move the ladders.

At one point, Becky was standing close to the base of Andy's ladder. He glanced down and must have gotten an eyeful of her cleavage, because his mouth fell open. His brush froze midway to the wall.

A big drop of paint formed on the brush.

"Look out, Andy," I called out.

Of course, Becky's head came up as she tried to figure out what I was yelling about.

The drop of paint broke loose and landed right smack on her chin. "Bleck!" she yelped.

I grabbed a rag and raced over. I swiped at her chin. She took the rag and rubbed the rest of the paint off.

Then she and I made eye contact and burst out laughing.

I looked up. Andy's face was bright red.

"It's okay," Becky called up to him. "No harm done."

She met my eyes, and I snickered again in spite of myself. In a low voice, I said, "If you hadn't looked up, it would have gone right down in there."

She giggled. "I know," she whispered. "Then he probably *would* have fallen off the ladder."

The task was soon finished and we cleaned up the mess. Becky tagged along as Andy carried Will's ladder out to the truck.

"I wish you could stay a bit," I said to Will. I winced a little at the slight whine in my voice.

"Me too." He gave me a one-arm hug as he maneuvered the lid onto a paint can. Then he let go of me to grab a hammer and used it to pound the lid closed.

I tilted my head to gaze up into his face. "Since Andy's got the night shift covered, I could come down to your place for a while."

He tapped my nose and smiled. "You've now got some white freckles mixed in with the ones Mother Nature gave you."

My stomach was a quivering mass of insecurity. "Okay, so I'll take a shower and then come down."

"Wish I could say yes, but I've got a second interview, at six, with one of the people from yesterday. It's looking real promising that I'll have a fully staffed force again soon."

I was trying hard to keep my big girl pants in place, but my lower lip had a mind of its own. It stuck out and even dared to tremble a little. I sucked it in and bit down to make it behave.

Will grabbed the paint can. "You want this in your shed?"

Shed was a glorified name for the eight-by-eight, rusty metal building with a leaky roof that housed my rakes and lawn mower. I nodded and led the way. Clearing a place on a shelf, I stepped back and Will hefted the leftover paint into the spot.

Standing close in the tiny shed, I put a hand on his arm. He took my hand and gave it a squeeze. He pecked me on the lips. Then he brushed past me and crossed the yard in long strides.

"I'll call you tomorrow," he threw back over his shoulder as he reached the gate.

I stood in the doorway of the shed watching him walk away, my mouth hanging open and my heart in my sneakers.

A few seconds after he disappeared, Becky came back through the gate. I headed for the deck and the bistro table where she was now gathering empty glasses and the iced tea jugs.

"I have a real bad feeling that I've just been blown off," I said.

She looked up at me, her eyes shiny, her usually smiling lips pulled down at the corners. "Sit down, honey. I've got some bad news."

CHAPTER SIXTEEN

Will called as promised mid-morning the next day. Standing in the backyard, I stared at the caller ID screen until the call went to voicemail. Then I pocketed my phone and went back to training Jenny.

The view of my freshly painted house blurred. I blinked hard, willing myself not to cry.

I'd bawled half the night, after Becky had told me that she'd seen Will out to dinner on Saturday with another woman. I'd had to pry it out of her, but she'd finally admitted that the woman was both young and beautiful.

I visualized her now in my mind's eye–an African-American goddess with velvety skin, big brown eyes and black, silky hair.

Okay, Becky would never be that cruel. I was reading between the lines of "She's black and kind of pretty and about our age."

Jenny pawed at my thigh. I praised her and gave her a treat. After all, she'd just responded to the cues I'd taught her that her future owner might be having a flashback or an anxiety attack.

With effort, I focused my attention on my job for the next hour. Then it was time to get ready to go to Ocala to work with Rainey and Lacy.

Lacy wagged her tail but otherwise her greeting was less than enthusiastic when I entered the Bryant home. She was lying under the kitchen table, at Rainey's feet, and *sans* her service dog vest, so her lack of enthusiasm wasn't because she was on duty.

"What's the matter with her?" My tone was probably sharper than it should've been.

"I don't know," Rainey replied in a worried voice. "She's been like this, kinda lethargic, since yesterday afternoon."

Sunny was at the stove, stirring something in a pot. "I think maybe she's allergic to something in this house. It's an old building."

I frowned. My house was built in the sixties. Their house looked more to be seventies or eighties vintage, not all that old as houses went. But mold could develop even in brand new buildings in the humid Florida climate.

Rainey must have misinterpreted my frown. "I'll move out if I have to." She gave me a defiant look. "I'm not giving Lacy up."

Sunny's spoon clattered as she dropped it into the pot. She took a step toward the table. "No, no. You don't need to do that."

She gave me a wan smile. "I've found an anti-allergy diet online. We'll get this under control."

I chose my words carefully. "Keep in mind that list of foods I gave you, and if an ingredient isn't on either the good or the bad list, check with me or your veterinarian."

Sunny nodded.

The discussion of food jogged my memory. "Hey, I misplaced a package of treats the other day. Did either of you see them?"

"I'm sorry," Sunny said. "I thought you'd meant them for Rainey. I put them in the fridge to keep them fresh." She went to the refrigerator and retrieved the small bag.

I took it from her and opened the top. There were only a few left. I stuck my nose inside the bag and sniffed.

Sunny chuckled. "Hey, if you're into snorting things, I can recommend something better than dog treats."

I laughed. "I was just wondering if they'd gone bad. These were the treats we were using the day Lacy got so sick."

Sunny's expression sobered. "Did you ever find out what made her sick?"

I really didn't have a definitive answer, only Doc Murdock's assumption that she'd been fed chocolate. And I was anxious to get started with the training, so I shook my head.

I slipped the treat package into my purse. I wanted to examine them more thoroughly later.

We took Lacy out into the backyard and began working with her. After about twenty minutes, she perked up some. Maybe Sunny was right and she was allergic to something in the house.

The rest of the training session went well. Rainey and Lacy were truly becoming a team.

When we'd finished, I sat down on the picnic table bench to rest a minute before heading for home. Rainey plopped down on the other end of the bench.

Now was as good a time as any. I launched into the spiel that Mattie insisted on, even though my heart wasn't in it. Lacy was Lacy to me. "You know, dogs aren't all that picky about their names. If you don't like Lacy, you could change her name. She'll get used to it in a week or two."

Rainey's head jerked around. "Oh no! Lacy is totally right for her."

I slowly let out the breath I'd been holding, then turned and grinned at Rainey. "You've really come along. I'd say another day or two and you're ready to graduate."

Rainey leaned back against the picnic table. "Thank God. I've got to get out of here."

That surprised me a little. "I thought you and your sister got along okay."

She ducked her head. "Yeah, we do, for the most part. But I really need to get my own place eventually."

Not sure what to say, I opted for silence.

"Don't get me wrong. I love my sister, but she can be a bit controlling at times."

I thought of my brother, Ben. "I'm a little sister too. I get it."

Her eyes flicked in my direction, her expression unreadable. She pushed herself to a stand.

I rose too. "You're doing great with Lacy. I'll be here tomorrow at one. That good for you?"

"Yeah." She gave me a smile that didn't quite make it to her eyes.

As I drove home, that blinkety-blank niggling feeling that I'd missed something was back. Yet again.

My phone rang as I was pulling up in front of my house. I pulled it out and checked caller ID.

Will.

My throat tightened. I let it go to voicemail.

But then curiosity got the better of me. I checked the messages. The first one said only *Call me*. The second one said *Got something to tell you. Call me.* His tone sounded serious.

The pain in my chest and stomach doubled me over. I rested my head on the steering wheel.

My God! Not again.

I prayed to be delivered from another philandering male. The gnawing ache in my chest said it wasn't going to be so.

I climbed out of my car and went inside.

Will called or texted four more times that evening. I ignored the texts and let the calls go to voicemail. I felt numb and raw at the same time.

At nine-thirty, my phone pinged.

WHERE R U?

Throat tight and eyes stinging, I called Buddy and Jenny back in from their last bathroom break of the evening.

Jenny headed for her crate, gobbled down her treat waiting there, and settled in for the night.

I flopped down on the sofa and channel surfed with the TV muted. Buddy put his head on my knee and whined softly. He knew I was unhappy but didn't know what to do about it.

"Neither do I, boy." I scratched behind his ears.

Searching for distraction, my mind landed on the Rainey issue. I was worried about Lacy. The suspected stalker was in jail, but I still felt uncomfortable about the situation.

I remembered the treats and fished the package out of my purse. Taking out one of them, I pinched its middle with my thumbnail. It was appropriately soft but solid all the way through.

To be thorough, I took the treats into the kitchen and dumped them out on my cutting board. With a sharp knife, I chopped each one of them in half. I sniffed the halves. Not a hint of chocolate. They looked and smelled perfectly normal.

The mystery of the missing treat bag was solved, but it brought me no closer to explaining how our ghost-like stalker had made Lacy sick.

Could he have hidden something tainted in Rainey's yard, maybe even the day before we were there? But Lacy was trained not to eat anything without approval. Had she gotten confused because I gave her permission to take treats from Rainey?

I considered calling Rainey and suggesting she check her yard. Maybe there were more such tainted goodies out there, and that's what was making Lacy sluggish again. But it was getting late. Rainey might be in bed by now. I'd call in the morning.

Back on the sofa, I analyzed each player–anything to keep from thinking about Will. I went back over everything I knew about Joe Fleming and then Scott Connors. No new revelations jumped out at me.

Rainey. Why did I have such an ambivalent reaction to her? Sometimes I really cared about her. Other times I totally distrusted her, and in between, I mostly felt bad for her. I thought about Jo Ann Hamilton's assessment. Borderline personality disorder would explain a lot, including my reactions to her.

And then there was Sunny. She stayed in the background most of the time when I was there, but Rainey's comment today bothered me. Was Sunny much more controlling than she seemed to be around me?

Joe Fleming certainly disliked her.

That dang niggling feeling was back. *Rainbow* popped into my mind.

The sound of a motor penetrated my brain, distracting me

from the feeling that I was on the verge of discovery.

It was past ten o'clock, on a dead end street in a podunk town. Who the H was out there?

Adrenaline shot through me. What if the stalker *was* somebody other than Connors?

I jumped up and ran to the front window. Nudging aside the drapes, I peered out, bracing for the green sedan I expected to see there.

My heart stuttered, not sure how to react to what I did see. A Collinsville sheriff's department cruiser was parked in front of my house.

And Will Haines was striding up my front walk.

CHAPTER SEVENTEEN

I opened the door as he was reaching for the doorbell.

His tense demeanor deflated. "Thank God!" He grabbed me and wrapped his arms around me.

I shook my head slightly in confusion. Meanwhile, my traitorous body was thoroughly enjoying the warmth emanating from his embrace.

I wiggled a little to get him to loosen his death grip. "What?"

He took a step back, but still held onto my shoulders. "Connors escaped."

I shuddered.

"Why didn't you answer your phone?" he demanded.

My brain went into total chaos. I wasn't about to admit that I thought he was with another woman. Because maybe he was. His worry for me didn't preclude infidelity. Indeed, I'd felt more and more like his sister recently. What the heck was going on?

I looked up at him, my mind blank, my mouth hanging open.

His mouth landed fiercely on my open lips, as he dragged me against him.

I was trying desperately to think. I needed to pull away from him for that to happen. My body stubbornly clung to his. He deepened the kiss, and most of my brain melted into a gooey blob.

But one crystal-clear part of it remembered that this man had hurt me horribly.

That part of my brain finally got my rebellious body to listen. I broke the kiss and pulled back a little.

Will's eyes bore into mine, his hands grasping my shoulders. "Why didn't you answer your phone?" he asked again. "I had to work a double today, or I would've come…"

His voice trailed off as I swiped the back of my hand fiercely across my lips. I wanted to spit to get rid of the taste of his kiss, but my mother's voice admonished that such a gesture was too unladylike for words.

"What's the matter?" Will asked.

I ducked out from under his hands on my shoulders and took two steps back. "Becky saw you."

His eyes clouded with fake confusion.

I knew that expression well and knew what was coming next. I braced for the "she doesn't mean anything" speech, the one my ex had given regarding the cello player he'd been bonking for most of our short marriage.

Why did men think that line had any merit?

"If she didn't mean anything, then why'd you do it?" I'd screamed back at my ex.

And as it turned out, she had meant something. He'd married her as soon as the ink was dry on our divorce papers.

Will stepped toward me and swung the front door closed behind him. "What the devil's going on, Marcia?"

"That's exactly what I'd like to know."

He lifted his hands partway, palms up, then dropped them back to his sides. "Are you going to tell me what Becky saw, or am I supposed to guess?"

"She saw *you*, with *her*." Despite my best intentions, I choked a little on the last word. My eyes stung.

More confusion on his face. "With who?"

"At that restaurant," I spat out.

"Ah!" His face relaxed. He reached for my hand.

I pulled back, narrowing my eyes at him.

And then he had the nerve to chuckle.

"Get out!" I tried to turn away but he grabbed my arm.

"The woman in that restaurant is my new deputy."

I stared at him, the words not quite computing. "Wha...?"

He loosened his grip on my arm. "Before I heard that Connors had escaped, I was trying to reach you to tell you that I now have a full staff again. I'm working a couple of double shifts this week, so that I can have everybody else on duty for a shift on Saturday or Sunday." He grinned down at me. "I'm going to have the whole blessed weekend off."

Again, my mouth was hanging open, and again he took advantage of that. He covered my mouth with his own.

The heat in my core spread outward like a wildfire. My knees melted.

He flung an arm around my waist and held me so tight my feet lifted partway off the floor.

Relief washed through me as it fully registered that he hadn't cheated on me. The dinner "date" that Becky had witnessed was an interview.

And then, for some dumb reason, I started crying. He broke the kiss but held me against him, rocking back and forth. "Shh, shh. What's the matter?"

"Nothing," I breathed out against his chest. "I'm just relieved." I leaned my head back and smiled up at him.

He used a big thumb to wipe the wetness from my cheeks. "Marcia, you need to get something about me. *I* don't betray the people I love."

My stomach clenched. Was he saying he loved me? I wasn't sure how I felt about that. My heart rate was already up there, but it kicked up another notch. I decided not to think about the ramifications of his statement.

"So can you shake free this weekend?" he asked. "Or do you have to do training?"

"I should work at least a little with Jenny, but I should be done with Rainey and Lacy by then."

His expression sobered and he took a half step back. Holding my hands in his, he said, "I don't like you going up there without me, not now that Connors is on the loose again."

"Do you really think he's going to stick around? If that were me, I'd be halfway to Texas by now."

Will grimaced. "Maybe. Depends on how hung up he is on getting back at Rainey Bryant."

I digested that for a moment. "He might be even more so now, since his Army career is over and he's a wanted man."

Will nodded, then his face fell. "I'll trade in those weekend days for tomorrow and Wednesday, so I can go with you to Ocala."

I shook my head so hard it made my ears ring. "No! We're going to have a normal weekend." I chewed on my lower lip for a second, thinking. "How about if I take Buddy with me? He's big enough to give people pause, and Connors doesn't know that he wouldn't hurt a fly."

Will frowned, his forehead furrowing. "Let's take this one day at a time. I'll trade Saturday for tomorrow and go with you. Both the Marion County sheriff and the Army are looking for Connors. Hopefully they'll have a lead on his whereabouts by the end of the day."

I nodded. I could live with that plan, but we were going to spend all day together Sunday if I had to tie Will to my bedpost.

Hmm, that was an interesting fantasy. I reined myself in and gazed up into Will's face. "Okay, one day at a time."

He leaned down and kissed me, a sweet and tender kiss this time. My nether regions warmed up all over again.

Then he let go of me and turned toward the door. "Okay, I'll pick you up at noon tomorrow," he threw back over his shoulder. "That good?"

He had his hand on the doorknob before I caught up with him. I grabbed the back of his shirt. "Where the H do you think you're going?"

A button went flying. He twisted around. "What are you doing? Let go!"

I did, but I grabbed his arm instead. "Will Haines, if you walk out of this house one more time without making love to me, I will kill you with my bare hands."

He held me by the shoulders again and looked down into my face. Then he broke into a grin. "I do believe you mean that."

I returned his grin and began undoing his remaining buttons. "After all," I purred, "there's no point in driving all the way home and then back again tomorrow."

I woke up early, to an empty bed and the fragrance of brewing coffee. I grabbed my robe and stumbled into the bathroom. A wild woman, with reddish brown hair sticking out all over her head, looked back at me from the mirror.

She had the silliest grin on her face.

I ran a comb through the hair but nothing I said to myself seemed to wipe that grin away.

Will's face lit up when I walked into the kitchen. He handed me a mug of coffee.

I took a sip. It was strong and black, the way I like it. "Mmm, I could get used to this."

He grinned, then pointed to the gap midway down his shirt. "You wouldn't happen to have a needle and thread by any chance?"

My face heated up. "Sorry about that." I put down the coffee mug and went in search of sewing supplies.

When I returned he was putting his empty mug in the dishwasher. That gave me a bad feeling he wasn't going to linger. "You can't stay for breakfast?"

He shook his head and took the threaded needle from me. He looked down and tried to line up the button. "The Marion County sheriff's got a lead on Connors. I'm going with him to check it out." His eyes crossed as he struggled with the button.

My stomach clenched but I kept my mouth shut. If I was going to date a law enforcement officer, I'd better get used to moments like these.

I took the needle and button from his hands and started sewing it on the shirt. Being this close to him, feeling the warmth emanating from his body, had things stirring inside. I gave myself a mental slap. Will didn't have time for fooling around right now.

I cleared my throat. "So how'd Connors escape?" I asked as I worked on the button.

"Don't know for sure, but they suspect one of his buddies on the base helped him get away."

I nodded. When I'd finished with the button, I knotted the thread, leaned over and bit it off with my teeth.

He lifted my chin and planted a gentle kiss on my mouth before I could move away. "You're quite multi-talented, aren't you?"

My body warmed all over again at the memory of some of the talents he'd displayed the previous evening. I smiled up at him. "Be careful, okay? I'd kinda like last night to become a regular thing."

He chuckled. "Me too. I'll meet you at Rainey's, around one. Don't go in until I get there."

"Okay." I shook my head. "Man, I can't wait for this case to be done."

"Me too regarding that sentiment as well." He leaned down and gave me a peck on the lips. "I'll call you if I've got any good news sooner than that." And then he was gone.

Mrs. Wells was waiting to pounce when Buddy and I came back from our morning walk. She stood on her front porch, arms crossed over her pale green terrycloth robe, chocolate brown eyes boring into mine. "Good morning, Marcia." No matter what, the amenities must be observed.

"Good morning, ma'am."

"Your young man has been around more lately?"

"Yes, ma'am."

"He stayed awfully late last night?"

That was Southern for *What the heck were you two up to? I saw him leave just an hour ago.*

I resisted the urge to grin. Even Ms. Wells couldn't dampen my mood this morning. "Yes, ma'am," I answered her.

A corner of her mouth twitched. She forced her face into a

frown. "What's that song that's so popular now?"

Actually, it had been popular seven or eight years ago, but I knew what she was referring to–the Beyoncé song. I couldn't remember its title but the gist of the lyrics was to put a ring on it.

I felt my own forehead furrow into a frown. How could I explain to this well-meaning woman that the thought of a ring made me want to run screaming into the nearby Ocala National Forest?

I faked a smile. "We're a long way from that step, ma'am."

Her face relaxed into a more sympathetic expression. "Of course. Y'all need to take your time. But don't wait too long now. You get too old, then you might have trouble with the babies."

I struggled not to let my dismay show. I had no intentions of making babies. I gave her another feeble smile and excused myself to get on with my day.

After a quick session with Jenny, I headed for Ocala. With Connors on the loose again, I took Buddy with me.

As I drove, the nagging sensation that I'd missed something was back. Only now I couldn't even remember what I'd been thinking about the evening before, when Will had shown up at my door and subsequent events had driven all thoughts out of my mind.

This was nuts! Now I was having a niggling feeling about my previous niggling feeling.

I laughed at myself as I glanced in the rearview mirror. In the backseat, Buddy tilted his head in his what's-up look.

When I pulled up, Rainey was standing next to her mailbox at the street, her back to me.

Lacy sat beside her in the cover position. She perked her ears at the sight of my car.

I looked around. No sign of Will. But Rainey had turned in response to Lacy's signal.

She waved with several envelopes in her hand. One of them slid to the ground. She went back to sorting the mail, apparently oblivious to the runaway envelope.

I got out and released Buddy from his safety strap in the backseat. Now I was really glad I'd brought him, since Will had apparently been delayed.

My stomach tightened.

Stop that, I told myself. I couldn't be going bonkers with worry every time he was a little bit late.

Buddy and I approached the mailbox. Lacy wagged her tail once, but otherwise she held her position.

Good dog, I thought as I leaned down to grab the errant piece of mail.

I glanced at the front of the envelope and froze for a second. It was addressed to Ms. Rainbow Bryant, and the sight of it brought the niggling feeling to the surface. Again, I felt like I was on the verge of some revelation. Trying to act casual, I handed the envelope to her.

She took it, then threw her arms around me. "Oh Marcia, I feel like a new person. You can't even imagine what it means to me to have Lacy with me. I hardly get scared at all now."

I gently extracted myself from the hug. "*That* is what makes me feel great."

I smiled down at Lacy. She did not break training, holding her position, but I swear that dog was smiling back at me.

Maybe now was not the time to tell Rainey about Connors' escape. With any luck, Will would be calling soon to tell us he'd been caught again.

"How's Lacy doing?" I asked.

Rainey's smile faded. "She's still a little mopey in the mornings, but then she perks up as the day goes on. Sunny thinks she's getting better because of the special diet she has her on. But I'm not sure Lacy really likes it. It looks and smells like pureed beef stew to me but she only eats about half of it before she loses interest."

I shrugged. "It may taste richer than she's used to. I'd give it a little while to see if she adjusts to it."

I followed Rainey, with Lacy prancing along beside her, up the sidewalk to the house.

A squirrel darted across the green grass and froze in the middle of the yard. I could never get used to how skinny Florida squirrels are. With no harsh winter to brace for, they didn't have the tendency toward obesity in summer and fall that northern squirrels had.

Buddy didn't react to the squirrel but Lacy turned her head and pulled a little in its direction. Rainey immediately held her hand down, prompting Lacy to touch her palm.

The squirrel bolted for the sweet gum tree at the corner of the house. Lacy ignored it.

Good girl! This time, I meant both Rainey and the dog.

Once in the kitchen, Rainey said, "Let me take Sunny's mail to her." Over her shoulder, she added with a grin, "Iced tea's in the fridge. Unsweetened."

A cold drink sounded good so I went to the refrigerator. The pitcher was on the bottom shelf, behind a stack of plastic containers of food. I pulled them out a few at a time and put them on the counter.

The label on the last container I pulled out told me this was Lacy's special food. Curious, I popped the lid and sniffed the brown goo inside. Smelled like beef. There were little orange chunks in it. I fished one out with my index finger and sniffed it. Carrot.

And something else. I sniffed again, then stuck my finger in and stirred. Sure enough, a tiny piece of onion rose to the surface.

My temper flared. *No wonder Lacy's mopey.*

CHAPTER EIGHTEEN

At the sound of footsteps, I quickly stuck the lid on the container and jammed it and the others back in the fridge. I was washing my hands at the sink when Rainey returned to the room.

"Shall we get started?" she said.

I faked a smile. "Sure. You up for an outing?"

A slight flicker of anxiety in her eyes, but then she nodded.

A few minutes later, I pulled into a shopping center parking lot and put my car in park.

"We going anywhere in particular?" Rainey said. Her voice was steady, no anxiety in it, just curiosity.

I hated to blow that, and I hadn't figured out how to say what I had to say. I tilted my head toward the big box pet supply store in front of us.

Rainey clapped her hands together. "I've been wanting to get some things for Lacy." She reached for her door handle.

I rested a hand on her arm closest to me. "Hang on. There's something I have to tell you." I was still seething a little inside at Sunny's carelessness, but I tried to keep my voice even.

"I know your sister means well, but she's ignoring that list I gave her of things that are bad for dogs. I checked out Lacy's food when I was getting some iced tea, and there's onion in it."

Rainey nodded. "Sunny said that was one of the things that's supposed to help with allergies."

"Well, maybe in humans." Although I'd never heard of that remedy before now. "But with dogs, it makes them weak, and that's also probably why she's not all that interested in eating, because she doesn't feel well."

Most of the color had left Rainey's face. She turned her head away and stared out the window, a muscle working in her jaw. Finally she said, "Sunny didn't want the dog in the first place. Tried to talk me out of it. Said it would be too much work, as if I were asking to get a puppy or something."

Rainey turned back toward me. "But then she went with me to the orientation about the service dogs, and that seemed to bring her around."

The orientations were presented by a member of the board of trustees–a real-estate agent who knew how to shmooze and put people at ease–not Mattie, for whom public speaking would be considered the worst kind of torture.

My brain had chewed through Rainey's words for a second time, and their meaning dawned on me. "Are you saying you think she's poisoning Lacy intentionally?"

Rainey shook her head and bit her lower lip. "No, but she might not have bothered to read the list you gave her." She looked away again. "Sunny acts like she's all careful and dedicated to doing things right, but it's her version of what's right. She can be pretty stubborn."

I took a deep breath to calm myself. "We're going to get some commercial dog food. Will you be able to stand up to her and insist she not feed the dog anything else?"

Rainey nodded, her jaw clenched.

I believed her.

Twenty minutes later, I was loading two thirty-pound bags of the dog food I use–one for me and one for Rainey–into the back of my car. And Rainey was cooing over Lacy in her new pink collar with fake rhinestones on it.

It looked ridiculous, I thought, with her red service vest, but I kept my mouth shut.

My phone pinged. I fished it out of my pocket.

A text from Will. *Where r u?*

At store getting dog food.
Connors got past us. B careful.
U at Rainey's?
Yes.
B there soon.
Btw, Connors right handed.

I pocketed my phone. So much for that theory. I guess the slant of letters spray-painted on a wall really didn't mean much.

We secured the dogs in the backseat, and I settled into the driver's seat and started the car.

Could this mean that Joe Fleming was the stalker all along? I shook my head. There was no way to explain away the bullet hole in his shoulder. Unless it *was* just some random stray shot.

"Earth to Marcia," Rainey said from the passenger seat. She was smiling at me.

I gave her a small smile back and put the car in gear.

On the drive to her house, I told her about Connors' escape from the stockade. My chest ached when her face once again paled. She chewed on her lower lip.

"Look," I said, "he's probably focused on trying to get away, not on you at this point."

She gave me a skeptical look and bit her lip again.

I cleared my throat. "What I mean is that I don't think he's going to try to hurt you now, not with the law being onto him. If anything happened to you, he'd be the first person they'd suspect." I wasn't doing a great job here. I hadn't even convinced myself with that little speech.

I took a deep breath and came at it from a different angle. "At some point, Rainey, you have to decide if you're going to live in fear, in which case the Connors of the world have won. Or are you going to hold your head up and take back your own life?"

She gave a slight shake of her head. "You're not the first person who's given me that lecture." Her voice was matter-of-fact.

"Sorry. I didn't mean for it to sound like a lecture."

"No. You're right." She sighed. "My counselor has said that

so many times, in a bunch of different ways. And so has Carrie." She sat back in her seat and squared her shoulders. "I guess it's time to start taking control of my life again."

I smiled at her. "That a girl!"

Her return smile was a bit feeble.

As I pulled up in front of Rainey's house, Will's car was parked half a block down. He jumped out of it and jogged toward us. His uniform was a little rumpled. It was on its second day of duty.

Rainey stiffened in the passenger seat. Was she worried about Sunny's reaction to his presence?

I had barely extracted myself from the car when Will grabbed me and pulled me against him.

What the…

He was holding me so tight I could hardly breathe.

"Thank God," he said. "You've *got* to stop doing that to me."

"What?" I whispered. I didn't have enough air in my lungs to talk any louder. What was he talking about?

Understanding dawned. "Will, I was just doing my job." I tried to keep the irritation out of my voice.

His body stilled. He held me gently away from him, his hands on my forearms. He stared into my eyes for a couple of beats, then nodded.

I was a bit shaken. Something had just happened, but I wasn't sure what.

A throat clearing. Rainey stood behind me, both dogs' leashes in her hand.

Will let me go.

I took Buddy's leash. "Thanks," I said to Rainey.

"I'm afraid I upset your sister," Will said.

Rainey shrugged one shoulder. "Yeah well, that's not hard to do some days."

Unease nagged at the back of my mind. But I had no time to process what it was about.

Sunny stepped out on the front porch of the house. She crossed her arms over her chest and scowled at our little gathering.

The uneasy feeling grew stronger. *Rainbow, Sunshine.* She'd changed her name…

"Rainey, may I speak to you, please?" the subject of my speculation said, but the tone was not that of a question.

I grabbed for Rainey's arm as she turned to walk away.

She turned back and made eye contact. "Bring the dog food." Her voice was firm. She headed for the porch, her spine ramrod straight, Lacy prancing beside her.

You go, girl!

I went around to the back of my car, Will following. When he saw my objective was to heft one of the large bags of food, he leaned forward.

"No. This could get ugly," I said in a low voice.

He frowned but then stepped back and nodded.

I grabbed the bag of dog food and wrestled it onto my shoulder. By the time I got to the front door of the house, I was a little pissed. The dang bag was heavy and bulky. The least Rainey could've done was leave the door ajar.

I lowered the bag to the porch's floorboards. Strident tones of raised voices came through the door, and I changed my mind. I was just as glad it was closed. I really didn't want to be a part of my client's blow-up with her sister.

But I wasn't above eavesdropping. I leaned closer to the door. And in so doing, moved too far away from Buddy for his ear perk signal to be seen.

His tail thumped at the same moment a deep voice said, "What are you doing?"

I jumped and whirled around. Will was standing at the bottom of the porch steps.

"Shh." I waved a hand at him and turned back to the door.

I caught the word *dog* a couple of times, and *sheriff* once. But mostly the words were muffled. Sunny's voice was definitely furious.

Rainey wasn't talking as loud as her sister. I couldn't judge her tone well. I hoped she was holding on to her determination to stand up to Sunny.

"I'll be in my car," Will muttered and walked away.

The voices had gone quiet on the other side of the door. I stepped back just in time.

Rainey pulled the door open. We made eye contact and she tilted her head in a nod.

I hefted the dog food bag again. "This needs to be kept some-place dry."

She opened the door wider and led the way to the kitchen. Sunny was nowhere to be seen.

Rainey pointed to one corner. "Put it there on the floor for now. I've got a plastic storage bin out in the garage. I'll empty the stuff out of it later and put the food in there."

I rid myself of the clumsy bag, and we headed out to the back-yard to do some training.

Rainey and Lacy were now working together like a well-oiled machine. I could've gotten away with saying this was our last day, but I like to give clients a day's warning that the official training is about to end. Sometimes they get nervous about flying on their own. This way they had twenty-four hours to get used to the idea.

Truth be told, the extra day was as much for me as it was for them. After spending hours a day for months working with a dog, it was a bit of a heart-wrench to let go of them. And Lacy was so sweet.

My eyes stung. *Don't go there, Banks.*

I called for a break, and Rainey fetched iced tea and two glasses from the kitchen. We settled at their picnic table in the backyard, the dogs at our feet.

"What's the deal with Sunny?" Okay, so I was curious.

My mother would have called it rude and crude curiosity. But I was still a little hesitant about turning Lacy over to this house-hold of neurotic women.

Rainey shrugged, seemingly reluctant to talk about her sister.

She was a blabbermouth though, with a poor sense of bound-aries about what she should or shouldn't say. I knew if I pushed I could get her talking.

So I pushed. "She seems upset about more than dog food and my sheriff boyfriend coming to the door." I winced inside, still not totally comfortable with the term *boyfriend*. It seemed so juvenile for two divorcées in their thirties.

"Sunny's a little crazy," Rainey said with another half shrug.

I let out a small snort. "Yeah, I got that."

She shot me a dirty look.

Note to self: don't dis people's relatives, even if they just did so themselves.

"Um, I'm not totally comfortable leaving Lacy here. What if Sunny decides to put her on another one of her diets?" The idea of that sweet dog getting sick again made *me* feel nauseous.

Rainey's eyes went wide. "You can't take her back!"

I put a steadying hand on her arm. "I don't intend to, but..."

Rainey shook her head. "I told Sunny that *I* would feed Lacy from now on. She's not to give her anything to eat, ever."

I patted her arm. "Okay, but promise me you'll stick to that."

Rainey gave a small nod, then looked away. "In some ways I was better off before she came back." She muttered the words, more to herself, it seemed, than to me.

"Came back from where?" Okay, that was just rude curios-ity speaking.

Her gaze flicked back toward me but she didn't quite make eye contact. "Sunny lived elsewhere for a while."

I suspected there was more to that story, but my mother's voice in my head was telling me to back off.

We finished our iced tea and I put Rainey and the dog through their paces one more time. Nary a hitch. They were ready to graduate.

"Since Will's waiting for me out front," I said, "let's call it a day. I'll be here about one tomorrow. Oh, and he told me that the sheriff's department will be sending a patrol car around fairly regularly, until they catch up with Connors again."

Rainey shifted her weight from one foot to the other and fiddled with Lacy's leash handle.

"Look, I know that's not going to make your sister happy," I said, my tone not all that conciliatory, "but the police presence should discourage Connors from trying anything, should he be hanging around."

Her eyes flicked my way, then she dropped her gaze to the ground. "I thought you said he's long gone by now."

"I believe that he is, but to be on the safe side..." I let my voice trail off, frustrated that we were even having this conversation. If I were being stalked, I'd want the police swinging by my house as often as they could.

I opted to let myself and Buddy out through the gate rather than go back into the house. I had no desire to cross paths with Sunny.

Rainey trailed behind me. At the gate, I turned to say goodbye, and for a dizzying moment I wondered if she was faking her own stalking? That would explain her resistance to police involvement.

She'd confessed to doctoring Becky's tea, which was a pretty sick thing to do. And she supposedly had agoraphobia but seemed able to go places on her own when she really wanted to.

Maybe Connors's early calls had given her the whole idea.

She was with me a couple of times when Sunny had fielded a call, but the voice sounded mechanical. No doubt, a computer could be programmed to make such a call, while one was elsewhere, establishing an alibi.

The pieces would fit together like that, if Rainey was even crazier than she seemed to be, if she craved attention so badly she would go to any lengths to get it. She was pretty needy, but that needy?

I stared at her face as a diabolical grin spread across it.

Then I shook my head, and Rainey was just Rainey again, smiling at me and saying goodbye.

Muttering that I'd see her tomorrow, I glanced down at the

white dog panting quietly beside her new owner. I was almost overwhelmed by the urge to snatch Lacy up and run.

CHAPTER NINETEEN

Will lowered his window as Buddy and I approached his car. "Done for the day?"

"Yeah, want to catch some dinner somewhere? My treat." I smiled. "Tomorrow will be my last day here, and I'm in the mood to celebrate." Actually I wasn't sure what I was in the mood for. Mostly I was restless and not ready to go home yet.

I expected Will to return my smile. Instead he ducked his head. "Afraid I can't. I, uh… I've got to get back to Collinsville. But I'll follow you home first and make sure everything's okay there."

That stuck a pin in any hope of a repeat performance in the bedroom tonight.

Once settled in my car and headed south, I tried to sort out my feelings. Regarding the end of Rainey's training, there was a mixture of relief, sadness and a little excitement. I was going to miss Lacy, but it would be really nice to finally get paid and be solvent again.

And I was more disappointed than I ought to be that Will couldn't spend the evening with me. I needed to get used to the idea that he was a lawman, and that meant there would be odd demands on his time, outside of normal work hours. He was going to get called out for emergencies, and he'd have to work some weekends.

Well, my schedule was pretty flexible most of the time, so I'd just have to work around his.

We pulled up in front of my house. While I was getting Buddy out of the backseat, Will climbed out of his car and came over.

"Sorry you can't stay for a while," I said in my most sultry voice. It didn't hurt to let him know what he was missing. "But I understand."

He looked at me, but didn't. His gaze was focused on my left ear. "I'd better check out the house, make sure Connors didn't come visiting while you were gone." He took my keys from my hand. "Wait out here."

I narrowed my eyes and almost blurted out, *What the H is wrong with you?* But something stopped me.

Buddy and I waited on the front porch for a good three minutes.

When Will came back, he moved around me, with Buddy between us. "I checked out back too. Everything's fine. I'll give you a call."

I grabbed his arm. "Hey, you're not leaving without a good-bye kiss."

His eyes went wide and his mouth fell open.

My own jaw dropped. Not the reaction I'd expected.

He shook his head a little, then leaned down and gave me a quick and chaste kiss.

"Nuh-uh." I planted my hands on his cheeks and pulled him down for a proper one.

His lips were stiff for a second. Then they softened and he deepened the kiss.

Heat shot down through my core. I expected his arms to circle me. That didn't happen.

He broke the kiss, but hovered close to me.

I stroked the front of his shirt. "You sure you can't stay for a bit?"

He shook his head, his expression now regretful. "Duty calls."

I nodded. "I understand."

He winced.

Huh?

He headed down the sidewalk, turning and waving when he

reached his car.

"Text me later," I called out.

He nodded and ducked into his car.

I pondered his behavior as I let a relieved Jenny out of her crate and led her to the back door. Buddy followed her out into the yard.

While the dogs took care of business, I opened my freezer and contemplated my choices for supper. After a moment, I closed the freezer door.

Again, I was feeling restless, let down. I picked up the TV remote, considered streaming a video for a while. I put the remote down again without pushing the power button.

I could take myself out to dinner, or maybe call Becky to see if she was free. But I was pretty tired. I hadn't gotten a full night's sleep last night, thanks to Will's attentions. I smiled a little to myself.

And then frowned. *What's going on with him?*

I shrugged. Men, even the good ones like Will, were a mystery.

One of the things Jo Ann had helped me sort out in our counseling sessions was the part I had played in the demise of my marriage. Granted it was a much smaller part than Ted's infidelity, but I had hounded him whenever he'd seemed preoccupied, insisting he talk to me. Jo Ann pointed out that most men need to be left alone when something's bothering them. They have to figure it out inside their own heads before they're ready to talk about it.

Of course, my ex wasn't real good at sharing things even after he'd sorted them out inside. Actually, I kind of doubted he ever sorted much out. I think he mostly reacted without significant cognitive intervention.

So kudos to Will that he knew when to go off by himself and think things through.

Feeling better, I again contemplated dinner options and decided to call the one pizza place in Belleview that delivers this far south.

An hour later, my stomach was growling loud enough that

Buddy was giving me funny looks. Finally, the doorbell rang.

I yanked the door wide. "It's about time." My mouth fell open. Will stood on my front porch.

With a huge scaredy-cat lump in my throat, I realized that he could've been Connors. And I'd just flung the door open without looking first.

Recovering myself, I broke into a grin. "Changed your mind?"

"Sort of." He ducked his head.

I spotted the pizza delivery guy coming up the sidewalk behind him. My grin widened. "Here's our dinner."

It wasn't until we were settled at my kitchen table, with napkins and paper plates and the pizza box open between us, that his glum expression fully registered.

"What's the matter?" I said around a mouthful of cheese, sausage and tomato paste. I was so hungry.

He gave a slight shake of his head and took a piece of pizza.

I bit another chunk off of my slice. Whatever was bothering him, he'd spit it out eventually. In the meantime, I was going to feed the lion that was grumbling in my stomach.

"I had a revelation today," Will said.

I nodded and kept chewing. The pizza was delicious.

"Those words you said to me, 'I was just doing my job.' I used to say them to Emmie, when she'd get all freaked out about the dangers involved with being a cop."

I nodded again. The lion somewhat appeased, I dropped the pizza crust onto my plate.

Time to pay close attention to what I suspected would be a serious discussion about his vocation. I'd already given this considerable thought. I was determined not to "freak out" like his ex had. After all, there are no guarantees in life. As my brother likes to say, none of us are getting out of this alive.

Will leaned forward a little. "Let me ask you something. How often do you get into these kinds of risky situations with your clients?"

Say what?

He shook his head slightly. "It's bad enough that I have a dangerous job."

Still clueless as to where this was going, I picked up a second piece of pizza. "I've been training dogs for a little over two years and this is only the second time that things have gotten dicey because of a client. Just so happens you've been a witness to both of those times."

His face relaxed some. "Okay, that's reassuring."

My stomach grumbled again. I took a big bite of pizza.

"See, here's the deal," Will said. "I think I'm falling in love with you and…"

My jaw dropped, which made the whole chewing thing complicated.

"Well, if we get married and have kids…"

I sucked in air, which turned out to be a very bad idea. A large chunk of sausage got sucked in too. It lodged in my windpipe.

"It'd be nice if one of us survived to raise them." He gave me a weak smile.

I tried coughing. Nothing came out, not even air. Worse though was that nothing was coming in. My unhappy lungs burned.

I tried mouthing the word *choking* to Will.

I must have looked like a beached fish because he chuckled. "I do believe I've left you speechless."

My heart pounded. *Breathless, dude, and not in a good way!*

I felt a nose nudge my knee under the table. Buddy had sensed my distress, but unfortunately dogs can't do the Heimlich.

I clutched my throat with both hands.

He laughed harder. "I'm glad you're joking about this. I thought you'd be horrified at the thought of marriage."

My eyes went wide as my lungs screamed for air. I tried to pantomime slapping myself on the back.

"What the devil? Wait." He jumped up.

He raced around the table, grabbed me under my arms, and hauled me to my feet. Arms went around me from behind. With his fists locked against my stomach, just below my sternum, he yanked upward.

The sausage chunk shifted a little. "Again," I wheezed out.

He yanked again.

More movement and a trickle of air into my beleaguered lungs. "Maybe harder," I whispered.

"I'm afraid I'll crack a rib." But he yanked a little harder. A brown wad of sausage flew out of my mouth and landed on the floor.

"Phew." I breathed in glorious cool air. The burning in my lungs subsided. A wet nose searched out the palm of my hand. I gave Buddy a reassuring pat on the head.

Will loosened his grip and let out an awkward chuckle. "Should've known even the M word wouldn't leave you speechless."

I turned in his arms and nudged him away from me, none too gently. "No, you lost me at the L word."

His face fell. "Well, I don't necessarily expect you to love me back, not yet at least."

I shook my head and gestured toward his chair. He circled the table and sat down.

I grabbed up the offending chunk of sausage with a napkin and tossed it in the trash, then resumed my seat. Buddy's eyes had followed my movements. He gave me his patented what's-going-on tilt of his head.

I wish I knew, boy. I gestured with my hand for him to lie down. He complied.

Staring across the table at Will, I tried to figure out where to start. "Number one, I think you've got the cart before the horse, or maybe it's that the horse has run away with the cart."

I paused for breath, my lungs still not completely recovered. I was pretty sure what I'd just said didn't make much sense.

I tried again. "You're right. We'd have to be pretty well established in the love department before I'd even want to hear the M word. Say in a year or so."

His shoulders hunched as if I'd hit him in the gut. But then he straightened. "You would consider marriage though? Eventually, that is."

I flopped back in my chair and rolled my eyes up toward the ceiling. There were grease spots up there. I really needed to give my little house a good cleaning soon. I blew out air and dropped my gaze again to Will's anxious face.

"I'm not sure. Honestly, I haven't really thought about it. You're the first man I've even been interested in dating since my divorce." He opened his mouth. I covered his hand on the table with my own. "And, Will, we've only been dating a couple of months. You're moving way too fast here."

He turned his hand over and clung to my fingers. "You're the first woman I've been interested in, too." He bit his lower lip, a gesture so uncharacteristic that I almost let my jaw drop open again.

The worry in his eyes made my chest ache. I squeezed his hand. "Getting back to the whole dangerous job thing. *I'm* just getting used to the idea that *your* job is dangerous. But I think I can live with that. As for my clients, they are, by definition, not always the most stable people. Some are recovering from addictions, some have anger issues. I've had a few have flashbacks right in the middle of a training session."

And they weren't always as innocuous as Rainey's hiding under the porch steps episode. One guy thought I was an enemy soldier he had captured and was taking back to his commanding officer. I opted not to tell Will about that not-so-fun afternoon.

"But all in all," I continued, "I don't think my job is any more dangerous than, say, delivering the mail or directing traffic. Heck, there's a certain amount of danger involved every time we go outside our houses."

Will's face relaxed a little more. "True. Even in your own home, a tornado can get you." He took a bite of his pizza.

I couldn't resist. "Or you can choke on a piece of sausage."

He snorted, almost losing his grip on his pizza slice. He fumbled it, getting tomato sauce on his fingers.

I grinned at him as he wiped them with his napkin. Having finished off my second piece, I was contemplating a third one.

He pushed his chair away from the table. "Sadly, I really do need to get back. I've been out of the office for two days–"

I put a hand on his arm. "Wait. There's something else."

He dropped his butt back into his chair, his expression a little apprehensive. "Okay."

I let go of his arm and sat back, took a deep breath. "About kids, I don't really want any."

His face clouded. "What?"

"I'm not fond of children." I couldn't imagine life without a dog around the house, but the thought of a kid constantly underfoot made me shudder.

His eyes had gone hard. "You could've told me that up front."

That ticked me off. "This *is* up front. We've only been dating what, eight weeks, and we've only made love once." My voice was probably a tad more resentful about that last part than it should've been, since I'd been the one who'd chickened out the first few times he'd tried to seduce me. "What happened to you getting it that I'm gun shy after a bad marriage? And why are *you* so anxious to tie the knot again anyway? I'd think you'd be wary too."

"Because," he said through gritted teeth, "I want a child. One that's mine, that nobody can take away from me."

My stomach roiled, threatening to give back the pizza. A boulder had taken up residence in my chest. His ex had a son by a previous marriage. When she and Will broke up, he'd lost all rights to even see the boy. I knew that had been hard for him, but I'd never realized he was on a mission to replace the kid with another child.

It dawned on me that this conversation might be the break-up one. My eyes stung.

I leaned forward and put my hand on his arm again. "Will, it wouldn't be the same."

He shrugged out from under my hand and jumped up. He

paced around the kitchen, more agitated than I'd ever seen him. "No, I know that. But my own child would fill this…" He turned away from me. "This hole inside of me. You can't begin to imagine what it's like, Marcia."

I could *begin* to imagine, but no, I wouldn't be able to completely understand. I gave my dogs up to their veteran owners on a regular basis, but I knew from the get-go that they weren't mine for keeps. Will had given his heart to that cute little boy whose picture he'd once shown me, and then the child had been snatched away from him.

"What broke you two up anyway?"

Will turned back toward me. His eyes were shiny. "She said it was because of the danger, that she couldn't cope anymore with the thought of that knock on the door that might come one day. But once we'd started the divorce process, it came out that she'd been having an affair for months." He smacked a fist against his other palm. "With one of my brothers in blue."

Ouch! That explained a lot.

My heart ached for him. "That's why you had to get away from New York," I said softly.

"Yeah. I divorced the Albany Police Department," his voice was bitter, "as well as my cheating wife."

"Come sit down again. I'll make some coffee. It'll help you stay awake on the long drive." I was praying that I could somehow salvage *us* out of the mess that the last half hour had made. But the sick feeling in the pit of my stomach was hard to ignore.

He stood in the middle of my kitchen, various emotions chasing each other across his face. Then he nodded and walked over to the table.

I got up and busied myself with the coffee prep. Once the coffee maker was gurgling, I fetched Jenny from her crate and sent her and Buddy out back for a final bathroom run. I was hoping against hope that I might convince Will to stay over. Best to have the animals squared away, just in case.

I went to the cabinet and got out mugs. Then stood, my back

to him, a fist clenched around each of the mugs on the counter in front of me. My eyes burned.

Who was I kidding? I had no business dating a man whose goal was children.

"What time are you going to Rainey's tomorrow?" Will asked, as if we weren't in the middle of breaking up. "One again? I'll meet you there."

My back still toward him, I said, "You don't need to babysit me." Surprisingly, my voice sounded okay. "I think Connors is long gone by now."

Despite my best efforts not to cry, a tear broke loose. I swallowed hard, trying to dislodge the lump in my throat.

Hands landed gently on my shoulders. I longed to turn into his arms and let him hold me, to feel the now familiar sensation of the world and its woes fading away. But tonight Will Haines was the author of those woes.

My temper kicked in. I turned and pounded my fists on his chest–even through a red haze, I had the foresight to let go of the mugs first. "Why didn't *you* tell *me* up front?" I yelled at him. "Why didn't you tell me that kids would be a deal breaker?"

He pulled me to him, crushing me so hard against his chest that my fists were trapped, unable to continue their abuse of him.

I started sobbing, which made me even madder. Pastor's brat or not, I would've sold my soul to the devil right then to keep from crying. I had promised myself I would never again care enough about a man that he could break my heart.

In all honesty, I felt far worse in that moment than I had when Ted and I broke up. With a growing sense of horror, I realized I loved Will Haines.

He kissed me on the top of my head. "I am so, so sorry," he choked out.

And then he was gone, his tall frame striding through the living room and out the front door before I could say anything.

I stared at the empty kitchen doorway. My throat ached. Reality slowly soaked in. He would never stand in that doorway again, nor sit at my kitchen table drinking coffee with me.

The house was too quiet, the only sound my grandmother's mantel clock ticking in the next room.

Buddy woofed softly at the back door. I looked through the screen. Jenny's tail waved in the air behind Buddy, a fluffy red-gold flag.

I let them in, and Jenny beelined for her crate, expecting a treat to be waiting. But in all the chaos, I hadn't put her treat in there yet. When I rounded the corner into the living room, she was standing in her crate, a hurt look on her face.

I really should make the treats more intermittent now–she was fully crate-trained–but I couldn't handle disappointing yet another creature this evening.

I got a treat out of the bag I keep on the mantel and tossed it to her. She wiggled all over and chomped it down.

I leaned down to close her crate door. Suddenly my legs were no longer willing to hold me up. I sank down in a heap. Buddy nudged my arm. I hugged him around the neck and cried into his fur.

A car engine revved out front, a sound one did not normally hear late in the evening in this isolated end of Mayfair.

Will? He's back!

I jumped up so fast I sent Buddy skittering backward. "Sorry, boy." I raced for the front window and shoved aside the curtain.

Mayfair's sole streetlight was in front of Edna's motel. The car driving sedately away from my house moved into its sepia-colored circle of light.

It was a green sedan.

CHAPTER TWENTY

I double-checked all the locks on my doors and windows, trying to tell myself that everything was fine. After all, the green car had been heading out of town. I looked through the front window to the now deserted street. Then I flipped the door alarm switch to the *on* position.

Becky wasn't likely to be in bed yet, but I texted rather than called, just to be on the safe side.

Hi. What r u doing?

Out w Andy.

Of course. Should've seen that coming.

I blinked hard and cleared my throat. My face started to crumple. I ground my teeth. I would not cry!

Have fun, I texted.

I considered calling my mother, but decided I wasn't up for that.

My body longed for rest, but there was no point in going to bed. I wouldn't be able to sleep. I considered streaming a video, but the noise of the TV might drown out the sound of someone trying to break in.

With all the lights in the house blazing, I stretched out on the sofa with my tablet and a throw draped over my legs. Buddy settled on the rug next to me.

I had trouble focusing on the novel I was trying to read. My mind kept sliding back and forth between worry over the significance of the green sedan and the topic of Will. During my more nervous moments, I even considered calling him. Broken up or not, he would come running to protect me.

But pride kept me from making the call. I needed to get back in the habit of taking care of myself.

After about twenty minutes, I gave up on the book and closed my eyes, praying I would be able to sleep at least a little.

I was yanked awake who knows how much later by pounding on my front door.

Will! Had he had second thoughts?

I jumped up off the sofa and almost did a header onto the terrazzo floor. "Coming," I called out as I disentangled my feet from the throw.

Reason returned and prevented me from just pulling the door open. I glanced out the window first.

Mrs. Wells stood on my porch, her hair a mess, her hands clasping the front of her terrycloth robe closed. She caught sight of my face in the window. Her eyes were wide, frantic-looking. "Help, Marcia!" she yelled. "The motel's on fire."

I flipped the alarm off and yanked the door open. "Stay back, Buddy."

Sherie Wells was already running down the sidewalk to the street. I pulled my door closed and bolted after her, grateful I'd never changed for bed, heart pounding at the thought of what we might find at the motel.

There were no cars parked in the lot next to it. No guests most likely then, so we only had to find Edna, Dexter and the dogs.

Flames lapped up the front of the motel. Hissing sounds could be heard along with the crackle and pop of burning wood. The sprinkler system was valiantly trying to do its job, but the fire seemed to be spreading.

A few townsfolk had gathered. I pointed to two of the men and Mrs. Wells. "Follow me!"

The nearest fire department was twenty minutes away. We couldn't wait for them. Knowing this, Edna had three heavy-duty hoses hooked up, one to each of her outside faucets, with the biggest sprayer attachments she'd been able to find.

I pointed out the first two, and the men got the hint. They turned the faucets open wide and started blasting the sides of the motel with water.

At the third faucet, I turned it on and sprayed myself with water.

Mrs. Wells figured out what I was planning. She was shaking her head, but she handed me a handkerchief from her robe pocket. I doused it with water to cover my nose.

She grabbed the sprayer from me. "Be careful, child," she yelled over the roar of the fire.

I nodded and bolted for the back door. So far the flames seemed to be mostly in the front of the building. I prayed it would stay that way long enough for me to get Edna and Dexter out of the living quarters in the back.

Dexter almost ran me down as I ripped open the back door. He had his aunt over his shoulder in a fireman's carry. "I couldn't get the dogs," he yelled.

"Is she okay?"

"Don't know." He ran past me into the night.

I ducked into the smoke-filled back hallway, clutching the wet handkerchief against my face. Still, my lungs burned.

Coughing, my eyes watering, I felt along the wall on my left. It was pitch black, which I took as a good sign. If I saw light, it would most likely be the fire.

The heat was almost unbearable. I came to a closed door, Dexter's room. The door was no hotter than the hallway, also a good sign.

Edna's room was across the hall and down another twenty feet. I shuffled sideways in the darkness until I felt the other wall. Not cool but not burning hot either.

As I moved forward, flickering light reflected off the left side of the hallway ahead.

Not good.

Edna's door was open. I froze in the doorway. The flames had licked their way through the old wallboards of the front wall. The flowered wallpaper curled and peeled as if it were trying to run away from the fire.

The drapes on the window closest to that wall went up with a whoosh, jerking me out of my stupor.

Whimpering noises from beside the bed. I ran toward the sound, praying the floor wasn't compromised by the fire.

Dropping to my knees, I felt around in the smoke and connected with a dog's head. A wet tongue licked my hand. Good, at least one of them was conscious. Grabbing that one's collar, I felt with my right hand for the other dog. I found a furry side. It was, thank God, moving up and down.

"Benny, Bo, you've got to come with me," I screamed, the fire roaring behind me.

Somewhere along the way, I'd lost the handkerchief, but I didn't have a free hand for it anyway. I managed to get my hand wrapped around both front legs of the unconscious dog. Hunched over, I started backing toward the door, dragging the one dog by his legs, pulling the other along by his collar.

But I had to let go of the upright one when I got to the doorway. We wouldn't all fit through it at once. "Follow me, boy!" I yelled, praying he could hear me and would obey.

My lungs felt like they were on fire. Eyes stinging so badly, I could barely see, I dragged the limp dog along the floor of the hallway. The smoke was a searing blanket around and above me, weighing me down. I tried to yell again for the other dog to follow me, but all that came out was a croak. I sucked in more air to yell louder, and almost passed out.

I fell to the floor, coughing, too weak to keep going. I had no idea how far I was from the outside, but it might as well be a mile.

Then hands were lifting me off the floor and leaning me against the wall. I could barely make out Dexter's plaid shirt through the swirling smoke. He leaned down and flipped the dog up over his shoulder as if he were a ten-pound bag of flour instead of fifty pounds of dead-weight canine.

Bad choice of words, my inner voice piped up.

I didn't have the strength to tell it to shut up, even internally.

Dexter kept a hand on my upper arm, pulling me along. I could barely keep my feet under me.

Worry gnawed inside for the other dog. Where was he? What if he ran back to Edna's room, the place that would be a safe haven in his mind?

A safe haven that was now an inferno.

A loud cracking noise behind us and a blast of hot air. Something had collapsed.

Dexter picked up speed. I tripped over my own dang feet and started to fall. He yanked me back upright. "Run!" He yelled in my ear.

We ran.

And then we were out in the night air–the blessedly cool night air. Dexter kept me running next to him for a good fifty feet.

Which turned out to be a good thing. With a loud whooshing sound, fire sprang from the back door and curled up the side of the building like a reverse waterfall. In less than a second the whole back of the motel was in flames.

Dexter let go of my arm. I dropped to the ground, gasping. He gently lowered the dog next to me.

"Take care of him," he said. "I'm gonna check on Aunt Edna."

I tried to roll over and sit up, but my oxygen-starved muscles did not cooperate the first time. On the second try, I was able to push up on my forearms to examine the dog next to me. His side was still moving up and down. His eyelids flickered on his mostly black face.

Benny! Bo had a wider white streak down the middle of his forehead and nose.

Where is he? I swiveled my head around, desperately searching, squinting from the brightness of the fire and the grit in my eyes.

I turned back to the motel, just in time to see the roof cave in.

Sparks flew in the night sky.

"Wet down the diner!" someone yelled. And the pathetically thin streams from the hoses were no longer making their futile attempt to stop the motel from being consumed.

Sirens wailed, now close enough to be heard over the roaring fire. The fire department had arrived.

In seconds the area between me and the burning building was swarming with figures in tan fire suits and black firemen's hats. Florescent yellow and silver stripes, two sets on the torsos of their jackets and two on each arm, glowed in the flickering light from the fire.

Hissing like a hundred cats, and steam joined the smoke rising into the air.

Mrs. Wells materialized out of the chaos of people and hoses and swirling wisps. She held a plastic glass in her hand. Kneeling beside me, she held it out. "Marybeth brought sweet tea."

I tried to laugh. It came out sounding like a straggled gurgle. Only in the South did the neighbors bring sweet tea to a fire.

But I took the glass and gulped the cool, sickening sweet liquid down. It slithered along my scorched throat, both stinging and soothing as it went.

It was gone far too soon.

"I'll get you another," Sherie Wells said, starting to push herself to a stand.

"Wait! Have you seen Bo? And how's Edna?"

"Edna's okay. The paramedics are with her now. And didn't you see Bo? He followed you right out that door. Dexter's got him."

"Hallelujah!" I flopped back on the ground. "I can't see much of anything right now."

"Tsk, tsk. I'll be right back."

I closed my stinging eyes and sent a prayer of thanksgiving heavenward. Moments like this both reinforced my skepticism about the existence of God, and made me hope most fervently that my parents were right about him.

A deep male voice from above startled me. Had God actually picked up the phone on his end this time?

I opened my eyes. A young man in a fireman's hat was hovering over me. He'd stripped off his bulky jacket. Orange suspenders contrasted sharply with the navy of his tee shirt. A logo with the number 18 in the middle of it adorned his left shoulder. "Ma'am," he repeated, "let me take a look at you."

I sat up and pointed toward Benny. Other than his heaving sides, he hadn't moved. "Help him first."

The paramedic looked skeptical. He had a small oxygen tank and face mask in his hands. He bent over Benny and held the mask over the dog's nose. Air hissed when he opened a valve on the tank.

Of course, the mask didn't fit very well, but apparently enough of the oxygen got into Benny's lungs. After a moment, he gave a small thump of his tail.

The paramedic kept the mask on his nose and glanced over at me. "How you doin', ma'am?"

"I'm breathing okay, although my lungs hurt. And my throat's raw." I rubbed at a stinging eye.

"Here, don't do that!" Sherie Wells's voice from my other side. She knelt beside me again, a wet rag in her hand. "Close your eyes."

I did as I was told and she gently swabbed over and around my eyelids. My eyes still felt gritty but not as bad. She began to wash my sooty face.

"Oh, Mrs. Wells, that feels so good," I said, my eyes still closed.

"Marcia." Her voice was sharp.

I opened my eyes.

She was smiling at me. "Don't you think it's about time you called me Sherie?"

I laughed. That also felt good.

CHAPTER TWENTY-ONE

I sat at my kitchen table, slurping down my third cup of coffee. My limit was usually two, but today I was desperate.

At two-thirty in the morning, the fire captain had finally declared the fire was "decaying." I took that to mean the worst was over. By then Edna had been transported to the hospital in Ocala for observation. Dexter had gone with her.

A neighbor had loaded Benny in his pickup and taken off for Doc Murdock's clinic. Bo was with Sherie Wells.

The captain, a tall, slender man with craggy skin and silver hair, had kept me there for another twenty minutes, asking me questions about the time the fire was discovered–which I didn't know–and how it had progressed.

"I think it started in the front." My still stinging eyes scanned the smoldering heap that had so recently been the Mayfair Motel. "I guess we're lucky to have gotten everybody out, with an old building like that."

My throat tightened. Had it hit Edna yet that all her worldly possessions were gone?

The captain shook his head. "Old buildings actually take longer to burn than newer ones. They built them with sturdier, denser materials back then." He dropped a large hand on my shoulder. "You were very brave to go in after the dogs. Foolish, but brave."

I shrugged. I couldn't have left Benny and Bo in that flaming building any more than I could Edna or Dexter.

I'd trudged home, stripped off my clothes and stood in the

shower until I fell asleep standing up. Then I'd dropped into bed like a rock.

But three hours later, a nightmare had brought me upright and gasping again for air amidst swirling smoke that wasn't there. I only dozed off and on after that, and was fully awake by the time my alarm went berserk at eight.

Now I was chewing on a cold pop tart and slurping coffee. I pulled a hank of hair around and sniffed it. Still a faint whiff of smoke. I yawned.

Hopefully I would make it through the day. I really didn't want to postpone the final training session with Rainey. I wanted this case done and out of my life.

A sudden thought made my insides clench. In light of the fire, should I leave Lacy with Rainey?

I picked up my phone from the table and called Mattie.

I filled her in on the fire and the green car, a piece I'd left out of my earlier summary of events.

"The car and the fire are probably a coincidence," I said. "An arsonist checking out possible targets in a town far from a fire station. Since I've basically finished the training and Lacy's with Rainey, there's no reason to come after me now."

I silently thanked the universe that the arsonist hadn't chosen the vacant cottage next to mine, then felt guilty about poor Edna.

Mattie was quiet for a few seconds. "How upset would the client be if we took the dog back at this point?"

"I'd say devastated."

Butterflies of worry for Lacy fluttered in my stomach, but I truly believed Connors was long gone. He'd struck me as someone who looked out for number one, first and foremost.

"I think we'll have to take the risk then," Mattie said, "and leave the dog with her."

I blew out a soft sigh. The butterflies still danced but the rest of me relaxed. I would get paid and would soon be solvent again.

I'd no sooner disconnected than my phone pinged.

A text from Will. Hope surged for a second, before I could

stomp it to death.

Heard about fire. U ok?

Ignoring the ache in my chest, I texted back. *Yes. At motel. No guests. Edna, Dexter, dogs ok. Building total loss.*

Tell Edna sorry. Glad u r ok.

Thx.

And that was it. The silent blank screen stared up at me.

Pressure built in my chest. In the past, he would have called. From his car, while breaking the speed limit to get to me.

I forced back the sob trying to escape from my throat. I was done crying over this man.

I knew that was a lie.

I took Buddy with me to Ocala, for company and moral support mostly. The car's air conditioner was going full blast, even though it was a beautiful spring day. Despite that, my eyelids kept drifting shut.

I jerked my head up, heart pounding. The turn into Rainey's development was coming up fast. I braked hard and made the turn, tires squealing a bit in protest.

A brick settled in my stomach as I pulled up behind a dark gray car. A familiar broad-shouldered silhouette was at the wheel. Will had come anyway.

Talk about mixed emotions. The green sedan and the fire had me spooked more than I cared to admit, but Will was the last person I wanted to have riding to my rescue.

I wanted to ignore him. In my head, my mother's voice said, *Don't be rude.*

He lowered his window as I approached.

"You didn't have to come," I said.

"Talked to the Marion County Fire Marshall." His voice was neutral, too neutral. "They're investigating the fire as arson. There were signs of accelerant on the front porch."

I nodded, not surprised.

Buddy and I headed up to the house.

Rainey greeted me at the door with a sly smile on her face.

"What's up?" I asked.

She held an index finger to her lips, and she and Lacy led us through the house to the backyard.

Once outside, she turned and threw her arms around me. "I talked to Joe this morning. He's doing really well."

I mustered a smile.

"He asked me over this evening," she said, grinning from ear to ear.

Glad somebody's love life is going well.

I tried harder to make my smile genuine. "I'm happy for both of you."

The training went smoothly, as I knew it would. During a short break, Rainey asked me to go to lunch with her one day next week. I'd known such an invitation was likely and had an answer prepared. I told her I'd have to check my schedule and get back to her.

That seemed to satisfy her.

I planned to text her this evening and tell her I was booked solid for the foreseeable future. I knew it was the coward's way out. But becoming friends with a client was an ethical gray area, and I had no desire to keep up contact with her.

Fatigue and worry for Lacy made my stomach a bit queasy. *Rainey loves her*, I told myself. I knew she would do everything in her power to keep the dog safe.

"Am I doing this right?" Rainey called out from the other end of the yard, yanking me back to the task at hand.

I'd instructed her to practice one of the last signals I'd taught her, and then I'd zoned out. I had no idea if she'd done it right. I cocked my head to the side, as if I were trying to decide how to answer her. "Show me again," I called to her.

She did so, correctly. Lacy responded appropriately, and I nodded, a forced smile plastered on my face.

"Let's call it a day." It was only three. I'd been there less than two hours, but I was done in.

I could see her face fall from thirty feet away. "So soon?" she whined.

I waited until she and Lacy had trotted over to me. Then I told her about the fire last night, leaving out the arson part and my running into a flaming building to save dogs. It was something only another diehard dog person would understand.

"I'm exhausted." Before she could say anything, I quickly added, "Hey, I'll text you when I get home and let you know about next week."

Yeah, I know. I was being a total jerk–throwing her a bone of false hope just so I could get out of there without a fuss.

The back door of the house opened and Carrie Williams stepped out onto the porch. Today's sexy ensemble was a snug V-necked tee in a shade of peach that should've clashed with her red hair but didn't and denim cutoffs.

I rolled my eyes, then pointed my chin in her direction. "Your friend is here."

Rainey glanced in Carrie's direction and waved. She then turned back to me, her hand still up, palm out in a stay gesture. "Wait here a sec. I've got something for you." She took off for the porch, Lacy on her heels.

Carrie followed her into the house.

I looked down at Buddy. "Dang, we were that close." I held up my thumb and index finger a half-inch apart.

He gave me his patented head-tilt look.

Afraid I would fall asleep if I sat down, I wandered around the yard, Buddy beside me. I drifted over toward the far side of the house, wondering if the painted words were still there.

They were. I looked up at the bull's eye on Rainey's window and shuddered.

Why hadn't they done something about the graffiti? It had been weeks now.

My gaze moved down the side of the building and I spotted a wooden door I hadn't noticed before. Doubtful it was ever used. Bushes on either side had grown partway over it.

I stepped closer. The window in the door was grimy with dirt and cobwebs. Curious, I leaned forward to peer through the glass.

Cardboard boxes were stacked shoulder height just inside the door. Beyond them was the dim interior of a two-car garage.

But it only contained one car–a battered sedan, with dull green paint.

CHAPTER TWENTY-TWO

My heart went into overdrive. I turned the doorknob, surprised that it was unlocked. Then I wasn't so surprised. Another piece of the puzzle fell into place.

Maybe Connors had been telling the truth. Maybe he was only responsible for the first few phone calls.

I pushed the door. It opened a few inches. I listened for a moment to make sure the garage was empty.

A short internal debate. The saner part of my brain said I should go get Will, right now.

If we'd still been together, I probably would have listened. But I really didn't want to involve him unless I was sure.

I put my shoulder to the door and shoved. The stack of boxes shifted a few inches, the bottom one rasping along on the cement floor.

Why hadn't I thought to question what vehicle Rainey had used to follow me to that Cuban restaurant? Or when she checked out Joe Fleming's address? I was a terrible investigator. The driveway had always been empty. Why hadn't I ever wondered about Rainey's car?

I pushed harder. The pile of boxes moved a bit more, and I managed to squeeze through the opening. Buddy slipped in after me.

The car had been backed in. I maneuvered around various obstacles to get to the back of it.

Buddy panted softly. The garage was stuffy from being closed up.

There it was, a Florida license plate, one of the special plates with a big gray sea creature in the middle of it and *Save the Manatees* across the bottom. And the first letter on the plate was a P.

As I turned back toward the side door, I almost tripped over a large plastic bin. I froze. Taped onto the lid was a piece of lined paper, the words LACY'S FOOD printed on it in big letters.

Slanted to the left.

Buddy sat down beside me in the cover position. I'd never signaled to him that he was off duty.

I didn't take the time to do so now. We needed to get the H out of there.

My gaze fell to the floor, to a paper sack next to the bin. What I saw through the little mesh window in the sack made my stomach clench.

Cooked potatoes were on the list of safe foods for dogs, but raw green potatoes or ones that had sprouted were on the dangerous list.

These potatoes had green skins.

I kicked the sack of potatoes. I might as well have handed over a guidebook on how to poison dogs.

Buddy's tail thumped.

I looked down at him. His hair stood at attention along his back, but he didn't break training. His ears twitched forward and he thumped his tail again.

Adrenaline shot through me. My heart skittered around in my chest.

Someone was behind me. Someone Buddy didn't like.

CHAPTER TWENTY-THREE

I wasn't totally shocked by who was behind me, but I was more than a little shaken by what she held in her hand. Her left hand.

She waved the gun at me. "You couldn't stop sticking your nose into things, could you?" Her tone was venomous.

A low growl rumbled in Buddy's throat. I held my hand out and his nose touched my palm.

"What things?" I tried to sound innocent. "I was just checking that the bin's lid fits snug. It's not good to have mold growing in the dog food." I faked a chuckle. "What's with the gun?"

Sunny shook her head and frowned. "You are something else."

That struck me as pot-calling-kettle-black territory but for once I kept my mouth shut.

"I thought for sure the fire would keep you away, at least for a day or two, so I could take care of that stupid little dog."

"*You* set fire to the motel," my hands fisted at my sides, "just to create a distraction?"

She narrowed her eyes at me. "I was going to burn *your* house down, but you never went to bed."

My stomach roiled. I'd left the lights blazing, afraid of Connors. And that had probably saved my own and my dogs' lives. But then Sunny had turned her craziness loose on Edna and the motel.

I ground my teeth. "You almost killed an innocent old lady and her nephew."

I didn't bother to mention the dogs, since she seemed to have no love for four-legged creatures. She didn't have much for two-legged ones, for that matter.

"Oh, yeah, like they'd be any great loss." Sunny snorted, her nose in the air. "She's just another capitalist pig, living off of the working people."

My plan, feeble as it was, had been to keep her talking until I thought of another plan. But she'd left me dumbfounded. Edna Mayfair *was* one of the working people, while Sunny lived off her sister's disability check, provided by the taxpayers, the rest of the working people in this country.

"You did all this." I waved a hand in the air. "Tried to kill Joe Fleming, terrorized your sister, made Lacy sick, just so you could keep getting her disability check?"

"No, you stupid fool, that's not the only reason. And I didn't torch the old lady's motel as a distraction." She smiled, baring her teeth. A strange light glinted in her eyes.

A chill ran down my spine.

"The fire marshall's gonna find *your* gas can and grill lighter from your garden shed back in the woods behind the motel." She laughed. "With your fingerprints all over them. No more Marcia coming to the rescue and saving the mutt, and you won't be around to train a replacement for her either."

My stomach turned over again. Did she think I was the only dog trainer in the state? I shook my head slightly. I was expecting rationality from this woman, when obviously reason had left for parts unknown some time ago.

I had to keep her talking. "What earthly reason would I have for setting fire to the motel?"

Her sickening smile morphed into a full-fledged sneer. "Jealousy, of course. Of her successful business."

Can we say PROJECTION?

The twisted logic told me a lot about her own motivations.

Get a grip, Banks! The goal wasn't to understand this woman holding a gun on me. It was to get away from her.

As I tried to come up with a way to do that, the door between the house and garage opened. I sucked in air, thinking, *praying* that it was Will.

But Rainey stepped into the garage, Lacy beside her.

"There you are," she said brightly, looking past her sister, who had her back to the door. Rainey held up her hand. In it was a small box wrapped in silver paper. Her face was that of a child on Christmas morning, offering her present to her mother.

My heart felt heavy in my chest. This wasn't going to have a good ending for Rainey, no matter which way things went.

"Go back in the house," Sunny ordered, her voice sharp. "We'll be in shortly."

Part of me wanted her to obey. Go back, before you discover what evil your sister is about to do.

Rainey took a step forward instead, confusion clouding her face. "What're y'all doing out here?"

Sunny shifted slightly toward her. "I said go back inside."

Rainey's gaze fell on the gun and her eyes went wide. "Sunny! What're you doing?"

I was distracted by the two faces before me, the one in front an older replica of the one behind it. A *much* older replica.

Rainbow and Sunshine... Sunshine had changed her name... because she had been born *before* the sixties.

"You're not sisters, are you?"

Rainey looked at me, her eyes huge, mouth open. She vigorously shook her head.

Sunny glanced back at her. "It doesn't matter now what she figures out. She already knows too much."

Rainey gasped. "Not about—"

"No, not that, but she knows I shot at that kid."

"What kid?" Rainey said.

"Your boyfriend," I said. "Joe."

Rainey dropped the present. It made a tinkling sound as something broke inside. She grabbed at Sunny's arm. "You tried to kill Joe?"

Unfortunately, Sunny was strong. Despite Rainey hanging onto her, she kept the gun pointed at me. Her gaze never wavered either.

"No, not kill him, stupid. Just scare him off. He's no good for you. I wasn't gonna have him hurt you again."

"Bull!" I said. "She's the stalker, Rainey. She wants to keep you upset so you keep getting that disability check."

Rainey dropped her hand from Sunny's arm and stepped back. "What?" She stared at me. "No, you're wrong. She's done some bad things, but she wouldn't hurt me."

Lacy must have thought she was having an anxiety attack. She pawed at Rainey's leg to get her to pet her. Rainey ignored her.

Sunny shook her head again. "You are so stupid, Mar-see-a." She exaggerated my name, the way the bullies in middle school had.

I pressed my lips together and resisted the urge to rush her. Eventually she'd get distracted enough, take her eyes off me long enough. I had to get to her before she could pull the trigger.

"There's a whole lot more at stake," she sneered, "than a lousy check. I'm not gonna let the pigs lock me up in some cell."

"Sunny, you can't just kill her," Rainey said. "That's m-murder."

Sunny looked back over her shoulder again. Her expression softened. "Go back in the house. Forget you even came out here." Her gun arm drooped a little. "I'll take care of everything."

Now or never.

I lunged for that arm, grabbing her at the wrist and twisting it backward. The gun went off.

Sunny howled, clawed at me with her other hand. Her legs flailed, trying to kick me.

I lost my balance and we went over, but I wasn't about to let go of that wrist. My life depended on it.

Buddy started barking. He didn't know why I was on the ground, but he'd been trained to bark for help if his owner went down.

The gun went off again. Someone screamed, a piercing shriek of pain.

Lacy's yapping joined Buddy's barks.

Sunny and I rolled around on the floor, our arms stretched above our heads. Her hand held the gun. Mine gripped her gun hand.

Suddenly she yelled, "No!" Her hand released the gun and she tried to push away from me. She somehow got to her knees, staring toward the door to the house.

I followed her line of vision. My heart stopped for a beat. Rainey was lying on the floor.

Dragging against my grip on her arm, Sunny struggled to get to her. I let go and scrambled for the pistol.

When I looked up again, Will was standing over Sunny, his gun in his hand.

And Sunny was sitting on the floor, clutching Rainey's head in her lap and sobbing. "I'm sorry, baby. I didn't mean it. I'm so sorry."

The dogs were still barking. "Quiet!" I yelled to be heard over the noise. They immediately stopped barking. "Back, Buddy, Lacy." I jumped to my feet and gestured for them to lie down.

Both dogs backed away in opposite directions and dropped to their bellies on the floor.

Rainey's eyelids fluttered. She opened them and looked up into Sunny's face. "Mommy…" Then her eyes closed again and her head lolled to one side.

My throat closed. Tears pooled in my eyes.

Will glanced at me. "Where's the gun?"

I held it up, pointed toward the ceiling.

He nodded brusquely toward Sunny. "Cover her." He reached down and grabbed Rainey's wrist. "Got a pulse."

Relief whooshed through me, making my knees weak for a moment, but I kept Sunny's gun aimed at its owner.

All the fight seemed to have gone out of her, though. She leaned, sobbing, over Rainey's motionless body.

My hand was shaking. I steadied it with the other hand. I'd never held a gun on anyone before.

Will holstered his own gun, then carefully moved Rainey's head from her mother's lap. Sunny resisted, but he grabbed her by the elbows and hauled her, none too gently, to her feet. Handcuffs came out and were quickly locked onto her wrists.

"You," he said through gritted teeth, "stand over here." He moved Sunny to one side. "And don't move!"

She stood where he'd placed her, still sobbing.

He glanced my way again. "Can you cover her and call 911 at the same time?"

I nodded and dug my phone out of my pocket one-handed. I told the dispatcher to send an ambulance and a Marion County deputy.

"The sheriff himself is already on the way," she said. "I'll send the ambulance."

Will had dropped down on one knee next to Rainey.

"Sheriff's on his way," I told him.

He nodded. "I called him when I heard the first shot, while I was running across the yard. Got him on speed dial now."

I had a funny feeling that was somehow a slam.

Will was examining the wound in Rainey's side. "Bullet went clean through. Gotta stop the bleeding."

Sunny sucked in air and shuddered. "Kitchen towels. Drawer by the sink." Her voice shook.

Will looked at me and gestured with his head toward the open door to the house.

I squeezed around behind him—no way was I getting within grabbing or kicking distance of Sunny, even if she was hand-cuffed—and stepped into the kitchen.

Carrie stood frozen in the doorway to the living room, both hands covering her mouth. Her eyes were wide.

I shook my head slightly as I set the gun down on the kitchen counter and started yanking drawers open. What kind of friend doesn't investigate when they hear shots, or when a strange man in uniform bolts through the back door and runs through the kitchen, gun drawn?

The answer was, not much of one.

The towels were in the third drawer I opened. I turned back toward the door to the garage and took two steps.

"Stop right there, young lady!"

It was a good thing I'd left the gun behind. An imposing-looking black man in a dark uniform stood in the middle of the kitchen, a pistol in *his* hand. I recognized him from the TV news–the Marion County sheriff.

"She's with me," Will called out. "I've got the perp out here, already cuffed."

The sheriff dropped his gun hand, the barrel now pointing toward the floor.

I raced into the garage and handed over the towels. Will used them to apply pressure to Rainey's wound.

He glanced up at the sheriff, who'd followed me out. "You got here fast."

"I was nearby." The sheriff 's voice was a deep rumble. He stepped over and grasped Sunny's upper arm. Her .38 was now tucked in his waistband.

The murmur of another officer asking Carrie questions in the kitchen, and her high pitched denial that she had anything to do with anything.

I stooped down beside Will, next to Rainey's inert form. "Will she be okay?"

He glanced up, his face grim. For a second, I thought he wasn't going to answer me. Then he nodded slightly. "I think so."

The Marion County sheriff led Sunny around us, but he stopped at the doorway. He gestured toward me. "This the girl-friend you been telling me about, who keeps getting herself in trouble?"

Will looked up at him, then turned his gaze to me. His eyes softened and his mouth quirked up on one end. "Afraid so."

EPILOGUE

I'd tried to come up with a good excuse not to come, but now I was glad I was here. Buddy lay at my feet, panting softly. Rainey had specifically invited him.

She was radiant in her sleeveless ivory dress and Southern belle-style hat, standing under a canopy of flowers in her back-yard. Joe beamed down at her with adoration in his eyes.

There were only a few dozen people sweltering on the rows of white chairs. The shade from the tarp above our heads only helped a little. An outdoor wedding in Florida during the summer wasn't the brightest idea.

I suspected most of the guests were Joe's friends. Carrie Williams was conspicuously absent. No doubt when the couple had compared notes, Rainey's jealousy had put an end to that friendship.

Good riddance!

"Who's got the rings?" the minister said.

Joe grinned and leaned over the white dog standing next to Rainey's left knee. He unhooked a small velvet pouch from Lacy's collar.

A low rumble of laughter from the man in the chair beside me. "Shh." I lightly smacked his thigh. Personally, I thought Lacy made an excellent ring bearer.

Despite some residual ambivalence about the woman, I was glad to see Rainey happy. Especially after learning how much unhappiness her parents had caused her.

Her hippie father had abandoned them when Rainey was four. After that, Sunshine had latched onto one slime-ball man after another. When one of those men wanted to move to California, without the encumbrance of a child, Sunny had taken Rainey to a neighbor's house for a sleep-over with their little girl, and had never come back for her.

Fast forward twenty some years, and Rainey had just returned from Afghanistan when her long-lost mother showed up on her doorstep, desperate for a safe haven.

It had only taken the Marion County sheriff a few hours to discover Sunny's true identity. Her fingerprints matched those found on the tape of the box containing the used paper towels. Those of the woman who, while in a drunken state, had run down a pedestrian in San Francisco. And then had faked her own suicide.

Sunny had lived under the radar for the past year, supplementing Rainey's disability checks by dealing in marihuana. The house was rented in Rainey's name, the car was registered to her. Sunny had no driver's license, no legal identity in the state of Florida, where she was wanted for child abandonment.

Both her false identity and her livelihood depended on Rainey remaining disabled and living with her.

The analysis of the treat Doc Murdock had recovered showed a pocket of concentrated baking chocolate, most likely inserted via a needle and syringe. We'd been looking for a stalker who'd somehow snuck up behind Rainey to substitute tainted treats for the good ones. But Rainey wouldn't have thought twice about Sunny wandering out into the yard on some errand. It would have been easy to drop the tainted treats into the bowl when she wasn't looking.

"I now pronounce you man and wife." The minister's words brought me back to the much more pleasant present.

The small group of friends stood and broke into applause as Joe enthusiastically kissed his bride. The guests surged forward to congratulate the couple.

"Come on, let's sneak out while we can," I whispered to Will.

He took my hand and we headed for the gate, Buddy beside me.

Halfway across the front yard, Will stopped and turned me around toward him. He kissed me soundly.

"What was that for?" I asked, laughing.

"For being good at your job." His expression was serious. "This case…" He gestured back toward Rainey's house. "It's showed me how important your work is. You give people their lives back."

My heart swelled even as a blush warmed my cheeks. I resisted the urge to shuffle my feet and say, "Aw shucks."

Will hooked a finger under my chin and lifted it, forcing me to look into his eyes. "I love you, Marcia."

Butterflies of anxiety danced in my chest, then migrated south to my stomach. We'd had a long talk two months ago–after that horrible day that Sunny had tried to make my last.

We'd agreed to take it one step at a time. Will admitted that he'd been able to suppress his craving for offspring, until he'd met me and the possibility of a new relationship seemed real. As much as he wanted a child, he now couldn't imagine having one with anyone else but me.

That had melted my heart and scared the crap out of me at the same time.

My ex had seemed a good match when we'd married, but then he'd turned out to be so blatantly wrong for me. My divorce had left me believing that marriage was little more than a crapshoot. But I was starting to get it that the success or failure of a relationship wasn't just about whether or not two people were "right" for each other. Sunny's poor example of how to love someone had taught me that you have to rise above your own self-interest and weigh your needs in the scales with your loved one's needs.

I didn't particularly want kids, but Will really, really did. So I'd told him I would remain open to the idea, for now.

If only he wouldn't throw that *love* word around so often.

"I, uh," I stammered. "I lo… I…" Inspiration struck. "I L you."

"Huh?"

I gave him a feeble smile. "Sorry. Sometimes, I'm gonna need baby steps."

He blew out air and shook his head, but his lips were quirking up on the ends.

"Hey, y'all!"

We both turned back toward the house. Rainey stood at the open gate, Lacy beside her and Joe just behind them.

"You forgot something, Marcia." She cranked her arm back and pitched her bouquet at me.

I jumped back in horror, letting it land at my feet.

Will chuckled and picked it up. He waved at Rainey. "Congratulations! Have a great life together."

Rainey and Joe both waved back. "We intend to," Joe called out.

I silently prayed that they would, despite the challenges facing them. Rainey was still far from being the poster child for mental health. But Joe seemed to know what he was getting himself into.

Will tried to hand the bouquet to me. I stubbornly kept my arms at my sides.

He threw back his head and laughed. Then he leaned down and kissed me gently on the lips.

"I L you too, Ms. Banks."

~~~~◇~~~~

AUTHOR'S NOTES

If you enjoyed this book, please take a moment to leave a short review on the book retailer's site where you downloaded it (and/or other online book retailers). Reviews help with sales, and sales provide funds for more books! You can find the links for these retailers at the *misterio press* bookstore.

Also, you may want to go to http://kassandralamb.com to sign up for my newsletter and get updates on new releases, giveaways and sales (and you get a free e-copy of a novella for signing up). I only send out newsletters when I truly have news and you can unsubscribe at any time.

We at *misterio press* pride ourselves on providing our readers with top-quality reads. All of our books are proofread multiple times by several pairs of eyes, but proofreaders are human. If you found errors in this book, please email me at lambkassandra3@ gmail.com so the errors can be corrected. Thank you!

As always, I am extremely grateful to my posse of critiquers and beta readers–my friend and cofounder at *misterio press*, Shannon Esposito who told me that I had "hit this one out of the park" (not so sure about that, Shan, but thanks for the encouragement); my wonderful daughter-in-law, romance author, GG Andrew whose eye for detail is so incredibly helpful; my brother, the official guy stuff consultant (who also thought this one was "the best one yet"); my sister author at *misterio*, Vinnie Hansen who critiqued and did a first proofread; my wonderful friend, Angi who is also my advisor on all things service dog related; and my final proofreader, my husband.

Also a special thank you to Clay Connelly, the Assistant Police Chief of Williston, Florida, for his advice on the workings of the county sheriff system of the state and how BOLOs are sent out, and also how they can go astray.

I have tried to be true to everyone's advice. Any errors are strictly mine.

And let me not forget my marvelous editor, Marcy Kennedy, who helped me shape the final version of this manuscript into the best story it could be. Thank you so much, Marcy!

Sadly, sexual assault is a very real and ongoing problem in our military. To me it is comprehensible–not justifiable but comprehensible–how in combat situations, a commanding officer may think along the lines that Marcia imagines in this story.

But far too many assaults happen on U.S. soil, at military bases and training facilities around the country. And there is no explanation nor excuse for them being ignored or minimized other than a male-privilege culture within the armed services.

Obviously, this is not okay. Women who serve their country should not have to fear being attacked by their own comrades in arms, nor should they have to deal with feeling betrayed by the very organizations they have sworn to serve, on top of the rest of the trauma inherent in sexual assault. I have known a couple of women who've had this experience and have personally witnessed their pain.

Hopefully the culture in the military will eventually shift to one of respect for *everyone* who sacrifices in order to serve their country, and rapists within the military will be prosecuted to the full extent of the law.

On to lighter subjects… Isn't Lacy adorable? I had so much fun writing about this sweet dog, both in this book and Book 1. Sadly we will now have to say goodbye to her as Marcia had to, but there will be more adorable dogs to come.

A word about the title, *Arsenic and Young Lacy*. As you may have guessed by now, all the titles in this series will be takeoffs on classic books or movies.

But my editor pointed out that she kept expecting arsenic to make an appearance in this story.

That had been my original intention, to find some way that the culprit could sneak arsenic into Lacy's food. But as I researched substances that were toxic for dogs, I discovered so many human foods that are harmful to dogs, and using some of those fit better with the story as it unfolded.

I took some liberties with the chocolate. It would probably take more than a few doctored treats to get the reaction Lacy had. But the symptoms she exhibited are those produced by anything more than a moderate amount of chocolate, especially baking or dark chocolate: vomiting, diarrhea, excessive thirst and agitation.

Onions (and garlic), even small amounts over time, lead to weakness, dullness and loss of appetite. Potatoes with a greenish tint to their skins contain higher than normal amounts of solanine, a toxic chemical usually concentrated in the green parts of the potato plant. Potatoes will turn green if exposed to excessive cold, heat, or light. The latter two would be easy to accomplish in Florida.

While it would take a large quantity of green potatoes to make an adult human seriously ill, it doesn't take nearly as much to harm or kill a dog. There are many more foods that are harmful to pets, so it behooves us to not feed any "people food" to our animals without checking first to make sure they are safe.

The towns of Mayfair and Collinsville and Collins County are fictitious locations, but Marion County is a real county in central Florida. Right in the middle of the time period when I was writing this book, the sheriff of that county was indicted on perjury and misconduct charges. An interim sheriff was appointed. His fictional counterpart is the one who makes a cameo appearance at the end of the book.

I am currently working on Book 9 in the Kate Huntington series, but I will be starting on the third Marcia Banks and Buddy book soon.

Here's a sneak peek:

The Call Of The Woof,
A Marcia Banks and Buddy Mystery, #3

Combat veteran Jake Black has always had a wild streak, which marriage and raising a child have done little to tame, especially since his wife shares his passion for motorcycles. But when he came back from the Middle East with a traumatic brain injury and PTSD, it looked like he would be sidelined... until Marcia Banks trained his service dog Felix to ride in a sidecar.

Being able to ride his beloved bike has given Jake the will to live again and to heal from his injuries, physical and emotional. But now his freedom and even his life are on the line once more. He and his wife have been accused of robbing a pawn shop owned by a friend of a friend.

Marcia and her dog, Buddy—who are at loose ends while their home is being fumigated for termites—jump in to help clear them. But myths and misconceptions about bikers, TBI and PTSD complicate the investigation. And Marcia's sheriff boyfriend is not happy that she's once again putting herself at risk, and taking him along on her wild ride.

~~~

And if you're a Kate Huntington fan, see the next page for an excerpt from her next adventure.

An Excerpt from ANXIETY ATTACK
A Kate Huntington Mystery

by Kassandra Lamb

CHAPTER ONE

The police radio chattered with unintelligible codes. Kate shoved a dark curl out of her eyes and stifled a yawn.

The uniformed officer in the driver's seat glanced her way. A corner of his mouth quirked up. "Don't know who said it first, but it's true. Police work is mostly boredom, punctuated by moments of sheer terror."

She flashed him a smile. "Sorry. It's been a long day."

What have I gotten myself into?

"All available units," the radio squawked. "10-31, shots fired."

The officer sat up straighter.

"Armstrong building, 2910 York Road, third floor."

Armstrong building. Why does that sound familiar?

Officer Peters hit the siren and lights, and the cruiser surged forward.

Kate's heart went into overdrive.

At nine o'clock on a rainy Sunday evening, the business district of Towson was relatively quiet. The few cars on the road quickly got out of the way. Kate suspected it wasn't so easy to get to a crime scene during a weekday, when these streets would be teeming with cars and pedestrians and delivery trucks.

Her heart rate kicked up another notch as they careened around a corner onto York Road.

"Remember to call me once you have the scene secured," she yelled over the wail of the siren.

Officer Peters nodded slightly without taking his eyes off the slick road in front of him.

He pulled into the parking lot of a high-rise office building.

Braking to an abrupt stop, he killed the siren and unhooked his seatbelt. The actions seemed to happen all at once.

Kate was impressed.

"Stay in the car until I call," he said.

The order was unnecessary. She had no desire to end up in the middle of a gunfight.

He was out of the car and running toward the building, one hand on his holster, the other keying the radio on his shoulder.

No doubt checking on backup, Kate thought.

She transferred her phone to her left hand and made a note on the pad in her lap. Going into an on-going crime scene by oneself would definitely heighten the stress level of the officer.

She'd no sooner finished the note than two other cruisers screamed into the lot. Their sirens ceased with a dying screech, and two officers–one female, one male–bolted from their cars.

Peters had reached the front of the building. He grabbed the handle of one of the big glass doors and pulled it open.

Kate thought that odd. Wouldn't an office building be locked up tight at night?

The other officers were hard on young Peters's heels as he bolted into the building.

Temporarily, Kate's moments of sheer terror were over. She sat in the cruiser, its motor humming, blue lights reflecting off the wet pavement in front of it.

Minutes ticked by. Mist swirled around the car, adding to the eeriness of the night. The yellowish glow of the streetlights surrounding the parking lot created mini rainbows.

Butterflies danced in Kate's stomach. What was going on in there? Her phone chirped in her hand. She jumped.

"Hello?"

"We have a gunshot victim up here. Ambulance is on the way. Come inside and hold the elevator on the ground floor for the EMTs."

"Sure, okay." She fumbled with her seatbelt release, got out of the car. More sirens in the distance, a different pattern to the sound. The ambulance.

She jogged to the building and entered the lobby. Stopping for a few seconds for her eyes to adjust to the darkness, she willed her heart to slow its pounding. It didn't listen.

She located the elevator in the shadows of the lobby and punched the up button. The up-and-down wail of the ambulance's siren was growing louder.

A ding and the doors opened, the light inside the elevator blinding. She stepped in and squinted to find the open-door button.

Her finger was numb from keeping it on the button by the time the EMTs were maneuvering their gurney and equipment into the cramped space.

"Okay," one of them said.

A frisson of panic ran through her. She couldn't remember the floor.

The older of the EMTs reached past her and punched the button for three.

"Sorry," she mumbled. "I couldn't remember."

"Ride along?" the EMT asked.

"Yeah." She considered explaining further but suddenly felt exhausted.

The elevator dinged and the doors slid open. The EMTs hustled down the hall toward a light in an office suite.

Kate followed them, her heart in her throat. She'd seen more than her share of the aftermath of crime, but she wasn't sure she was up for this tonight.

A security guard inside the lighted offices let the EMTs pass but held up a hand to stop her.

"I'm with Officer Peters," she said. "Doing a ride-along for the governor's task force on PTSD in police officers. I need to observe the officers in action."

"Sorry, ma'am. This is a restricted area."

"But I need to observe the officers in action. I won't do anything to contaminate the crime scene."

"That's not my worry, ma'am. We have top secret projects

here."

Movement in the corner of her eye. She turned her head.

A stocky man of medium height was pushing through the glass doors into the oversized reception area. He wore a business suit but carried himself like a police officer. Pulling back his suit jacket to expose a gold badge attached to his belt, he said, "Detective Russell."

The detective looked from the guard to Kate and back again. "What's going on?" He glanced past her to a light in one of the darkened hallways leading off from the reception area.

Kate jumped in before the guard could answer. "I'm with Officer Peters. I need to be at the crime scene."

Detective Russell raised an eyebrow. "You a witness?"

"Yes." It wasn't a total lie. She'd witnessed the call.

He grabbed her elbow. "Come with me."

The guard seemed to hesitate, then stepped aside.

They walked briskly down the dark hallway. Rounding a corner, they entered a long room, the source of the light. Its walls were flanked by Formica workbenches, with computer monitors scattered along them, all dark.

Officer Peters stood at parade rest about a third of the way down the room. He held a small book in his hands.

The detective let go of her arm and again flipped his jacket aside to show his badge. "Russell."

Peters wrote in the book, checked his watch, wrote the time.

"What's the deal?" Russell said.

The officer started filling him in.

Kate stepped to one side to see past him, then froze. Her heart skittered around in her chest. She blinked and looked again at the man lying on the floor, the EMTs working with quick, efficient movements to stop the blood spurting from his chest.

A scream erupted unbidden from her throat.

Officer Peters pivoted toward her. "Mrs. Huntington, please. Go out in the hall."

His words barely registered in her brain, which was still trying to compute what her eyes were seeing. "My God, Manny!" Her hands flew to her mouth to stifle another scream.

"You know him?" Detective Russell said.

She nodded, willing herself not to faint. "Y-yes," she stammered. "He's M-manny. Manuel Ortiz. He works for my husband."

~~~~~~~~~

ABOUT THE AUTHOR

Kassandra Lamb has never been able to decide which she loves more, psychology or writing. In college, she realized that writers need a day job in order to eat, so she studied psychology. After a career as a psychotherapist and college professor, she is now retired and can pursue her passion for writing. She spends most of her time in an alternate universe with her characters. The portal to this universe, aka her computer, is located in Florida, where her husband and dog catch occasional glimpses of her. She and her husband spend part of each summer in her native Maryland, where her Kate Huntington series is based.

Kass is currently working on Book 9 of the Kate Huntington mystery series and Book 3 of the Marcia Banks and Buddy cozy mysteries. She also has four novellas out in the Kate on Vacation series (lighter reads along the lines of cozy mysteries but with the same main characters as the Kate Huntington series).

To read and see more about Kassandra and her characters you can go to http://kassandralamb.com. Be sure to sign up for the newsletter there to get a heads up about new releases, plus special offers and bonuses for subscribers. (New subscribers get a free e-copy of the first Kate on Vacation novella.)

Kass's e-mail is lambkassandra3@gmail.com and she loves hearing from readers! She's also on Facebook (https://www.facebook.com/kassandralambauthor) and hangs out some on Twitter @KassandraLamb. She blogs about psychological topics and other random things at http://misteriopress.com.

Please check out these other great *misterio press* series:

Mulitple Motives (Kate Huntington Mysteries)
by Kassandra Lamb

Karma's A Bitch (Pet Psychic Mysteries)
by Shannon Esposito

Maui Widow Waltz (Islands of Aloha Mysteries)
by JoAnn Bassett

The Metaphysical Detective (Riga Hayworth Mysteries)
by Kirsten Weiss

Dangerous and Unseemly (Concordia Wells Mysteries)
by K.B. Owen

Murder, Honey (Carol Sabala Mysteries)
by Vinnie Hansen

**Steam and Sensibility
(Sensibility Grey Steampunk Mysteries)**
by Kirsten Weiss

Made in the USA
San Bernardino, CA
27 January 2017